# Love and Harmony

## The Abundance Series
## Book 1.5

### Contemporary Christian Romance

.

## SALLY BAYLESS

## Kimberlin Belle Publishing

Printed in the United States of America
First Printing, 2016
ISBN: 978-1-946034-02-1

Kimberlin Belle Publishing
Contact: admin@kimberlinbelle.com

All Scripture quotations, unless otherwise indicated, are taken from the Holy Bible, New International Version®, NIV®. Copyright ©1973, 1978, 1984, 2011 by Biblica, Inc.™ Used by permission of Zondervan. All rights reserved worldwide. www.zondervan.com The "NIV" and "New International Version" are trademarks registered in the United States Patent and Trademark Office by Biblica, Inc.™

Scripture quotations from THE MESSAGE. Copyright © by Eugene H. Peterson 1993, 1994, 1995, 1996, 2000, 2001, 2002. Used by permission of NavPress. All rights reserved. Represented by Tyndale House Publishers, Inc.

Publisher's Note: This is a work of fiction. Names, characters, places, and incidents are a product of the author's imagination. Locales and public names are sometimes used for atmospheric purposes. Any resemblance to actual people, living or dead, or to businesses, companies, events, institutions, or locales is completely coincidental.

Cover Design by The Killion Group, Inc.

# Chapter One

With every new calendar year and every new school semester came a chance to begin again, to become the person you were meant to be. Or the person you once had been but somehow lost.

Yep. Seth Williams nodded. Today, January 7, was the first day of a new semester at a new high school, and it was time for Tony, his half-brother, to get back on track.

Seth was starting over as well. His new job as interim principal at Tony's school meant big challenges, but they were challenges he was willing to face if it meant Tony might get his life straightened out. Stepping in mid-year—after the previous principal, his secretary, and the athletic director had been fired for misappropriating funds—would require flexibility, which was not Seth's strongest suit.

He rose from his desk, straightened his tie, and walked out of his office, right into a stampede. Only worse. In a stampede, all the cattle headed the same way. Here, kids plowed four directions at once, and the beige concrete-block walls reverberated with loud conversations and the clang of lockers.

"Is that the new principal?" a red-headed girl said.

"He kind of looks like we should salute, doesn't he?" replied a girl who had to be her twin. Both wore too much makeup and showed too much skin for a northern Missouri school day in winter—or, really, a school day in any season.

He ignored the twins—for now. But they were in for a rude awakening during the third-period assembly, when he would introduce himself to the student body and set forth some straight-forward rules, starting with a dress code.

Call him old-fashioned, but Seth had made it clear to the school board that if he ran the high school, things would change. He wouldn't promote the "Christian values" one board member had suggested, but he would expect the students to show respect for themselves and for others.

He passed the twins and almost collided with a boy carrying a tuba case.

The boy detoured around him.

Seth pulled his phone from his pocket and checked the time. Five minutes until the bell and still no text from Tony.

After much begging, Tony had been allowed to drive to school in the ancient pickup truck Seth had bought him as a gift for his sixteenth birthday, a symbol that Seth really believed Tony was going to make a fresh start. But if Tony didn't text to say he'd arrived, tomorrow he could come in an hour early with Seth or ride the bus.

Seth shoved the phone back in his pocket.

Twenty feet ahead, the hallway made a T. From down to the right, someone let out a gleeful cry—"Fight!"

A second later, a chant began, the students sounding as bloodthirsty as the Romans at the Coliseum. "Fight. Fight. Fight."

Seth set his jaw, hurried around the corner, and looked over the students' heads. A beefy blond kid was holding a dark-haired boy on the floor and landing solid punches.

Students ringed the pair, but teachers from the nearby classrooms were nowhere to be seen.

Seth pulled a police whistle from the pocket of his khakis and blew on it long and hard. "Break it up!" he shouted. "Now." He pushed his way through a trio of girls in leggings and T-shirts.

The blond boy paused, fist raised, and looked at Seth with wide eyes.

The dark-haired kid took the opportunity to slam a punch into his opponent's nose.

Seth gritted his teeth. The past week had been so quiet as he settled into his office and prepared for the semester. He'd only rarely seen a student pass through the halls for basketball practice.

That honeymoon was over.

He grabbed each of the boys by the arm and yanked them to their feet.

The blond slumped, head down.

The dark-haired boy spun toward Seth with his jaw clenched and his fists tight. Then the kid looked up.

Way up.

At six-four, close to two hundred pounds, and still mostly muscle from his days in the Navy, Seth could break up most fights with one glance.

The boy was tall but thin, no match for Seth. The kid lowered his fists. His square jaw, though, didn't relax.

A jaw that looked exactly like that of Seth's boss, Superintendent Roscoe Grange.

"Boys, I'm your new principal, Mr. Williams," Seth said. "And you are?"

"Johnny Driscoll," the blond mumbled.

"J.W. Grange," the dark-haired one said with a note of defiance.

Just as Seth had feared. Suspending the superintendent's grandson on the first day of class was not the best way to start a new job.

A group of girls whispered, and one pointed down the hall.

Roscoe Grange was walking straight toward them. Familiar square jaw, buzz-cut gray hair, unreadable steel-blue eyes.

Seth's chest tightened. He couldn't guess how the man would react, so Seth had to go with his gut. Which said that this group of high school students shared several traits with a pack of wild dogs. There might be consequences later from Roscoe, but Seth had to show he was in charge. "My office after school for detention," he said to the boys. "One hour, every day this week."

Johnny nodded.

"But I can't miss basketball practice." J.W. glanced toward his grandfather. His voice rang with an assurance that he was above the rules.

"I'm seeing your coach later this morning," Seth said. "I'll explain that you'll be late. Be grateful it's my first day. Once we go over the new student handbook during the assembly, fighting will get you an automatic two-week suspension. Understood?"

"Understood," Johnny said.

J.W. shot a look at Roscoe, his eyes hopeful.

Seth glanced at Roscoe as well. He really didn't want to have to find out if his old job teaching Advanced Placement Physics was still available in Tennessee.

Roscoe's bushy gray eyebrows pulled together. He glared at J.W. and shook his head, once right, once left.

J.W.'s face fell. "Understood," he said to Seth.

Roscoe walked over to Seth and said under his breath, "You're doing fine."

Seth's chest relaxed. "Thank you, sir." He turned to the two boys. "You stay here. The rest of you, get to class."

"I left those papers we talked about on your desk," Roscoe said. Without another word, he left.

Seth took the boys to his office, determined that their fight was caused more by hot heads than by a significant issue, and sent them to class.

One crisis resolved.

And he hadn't been fired. He still had a shot at making this interim position a permanent job.

He checked his phone again. Still no word from his brother.

But Tony hadn't been one of the boys fighting. That was a plus. And if he had a problem driving, Seth would have heard. Maybe the kid was nervous, being at a new school, and forgot to text.

Seth could wander down the hall and take a peek in his brother's homeroom.

No, that wouldn't go over well. Too controlling.

He forced himself to take a deep breath and let it out deliberately. He needed to relax. Everything was fine.

☙

A loud metallic crunch, followed by a *clinkle*, echoed across the parking lot.

Becky Hamlin stopped at the doors of the Abundance Community Church and squinted back over her shoulder, into the winter-white sun, at her car.

Just past the side yard of the church, in the lot it shared with Abundance High School, a full-size pickup was stuck to the front bumper of her cute little blue Toyota. After a few seconds, the truck backed up slightly and stopped. The vehicle, once green, sported some white replacement body parts and had seen better days. The crash, however, appeared to have barely scratched it.

And the tall, blond boy climbing out appeared unharmed.

"Are you all right?" She retraced her steps along the icy sidewalk until she reached the parking lot.

"Yeah, I'm fine, but"—his voice grew thin and nervous—"I'm sorry about your car."

Becky hurried over. So much for being on time to her meeting. She'd even gotten up half an hour early to go through the new drive-thru donut place to get Pastor Corey's favorite, a sour cream cake donut. And of course, a donut for herself, which she'd accidentally already eaten.

"I can't believe I did this," the boy said. "I was late and—"

"Let's see how bad it is before we get too upset." She bent down and checked her front-passenger-side headlight.

Completely shattered.

Pretty much how the boy looked.

She stood, brushed some flecks of powdered sugar off her red coat, and looked down at a baggie caught on a crack in the pavement.

A baggie that held what looked like a tiny bit of pot. Inexperienced drivers weren't the only downside of the church sharing a parking lot with the high school. Pastor Corey had shown an educational video so the whole church staff could understand the drug problem.

At least the pot didn't seem to belong to the kid who'd just hit her car.

She turned to the boy. "I'm Becky Hamlin."

"Tony Williams." He glanced at her Toyota and zipped up his gray jacket.

"These things happen," she said. "We just need to exchange insurance information."

He leaned into the truck and returned with a brand-new notebook, a pen, and an insurance card. A minute later, he handed her a sheet of paper that he'd carefully ripped along the perforations. "I wrote it all down, like they taught us in driver's ed."

"Thank you." Tony sure was polite. And, though she didn't think she'd met him before, there was something familiar about him. She used his notebook and pen to write down her information.

The first-period bell rang at Abundance High, loud and clear in the parking lot. The private school forty miles south in Columbia, where she taught music, might not return from winter break until tomorrow, but the Abundance public schools were back in session.

"You'd better get to class now," she said. "I'll call your folks later."

"It's my brother. He should be here any minute. I texted him. He's coming over from the high school."

Becky scanned what the boy had written down. Tony and...*Seth Williams?* She looked at the boy more closely. No wonder he seemed so familiar. "All right. I'll wait." Despite the circumstances, a tingle of excitement zipped through her heart. She'd read in the paper that Seth had taken a job in Abundance, but she hadn't seen him since all those years ago at church camp. And now...

Clearly today had been the perfect day to wear her new red coat. The color set off her dark hair and brown eyes and matched the red boots she'd found on clearance.

"I read about your brother in the paper." Becky pulled her hair out from where it was caught inside her scarf. "New principal, huh?"

"Yeah." He leaned against the truck, and his face tightened as if his stomach hurt. "That's my brother, My-Way-or-the-Highway Williams."

"Oh." *My-Way-or-the-Highway?* That was not the Seth she'd known. "And you just moved to town?"

"Yeah."

Poor Tony. Today must be his first day at a new school.

"The kids here are going to love me." Tony's words were thick with sarcasm. "Everybody wants to be friends with the principal's brother."

She gave him a sympathetic smile and peeked at her phone. Her meeting with Corey should have started about the time that bell rang. He had the local ecumenical leaders' breakfast at nine, but had said if she came in at eight thirty, they could talk for fifteen minutes. She slid off her right glove, decided it was too cold to take off the other one, and awkwardly tapped out a text with one finger. Not her usual *Sorry, running a bit late* because she'd gotten too caught up talking with someone, but *Someone hit my car. Be there soon. Can't wait to tell you my idea.*

An idea she thought was brilliant. The perfect way to make up for how she'd let the town down. And it might even help her land her dream job—teaching music in the Abundance public schools.

"There." Tony pointed.

A man in a navy ski jacket strode across the parking lot from the high school.

From a distance, he looked a bit like her cousin Jack. Brown hair and a beard. And tall. The man walking toward her had to be over six feet and had shoulders like a football player. The Seth she'd known had been fifteen, skinny, and barely taller than her own 5'3". It didn't matter. She'd have recognized him anywhere.

"Tony." Seth's voice was deeper but still familiar. "How bad is it?"

Tony winced and gestured to her car. "I gave her the insurance information and your cell number. And got hers."

Seth took the paper Tony offered, glanced at the two vehicles, and turned toward her.

She stood up straighter, glad the red boots had heels, and tried to suck in the five pounds she'd gained since the new donut shop opened.

"Seth Williams." He shook her hand, then looked down toward the plastic baggie in the pothole. He jerked his head toward his brother.

Seth had barely looked at her.

Of course he'd be more concerned about his brother if he thought the boy might be involved with drugs. But Tony didn't smell like pot.

"I'm sorry," Seth said, now facing her. "I'll call our insurance company as soon as I get out of my first meeting. I thought he was doing okay driving, but...I take full responsibility, ma'am."

Ma'am? Becky's heart shriveled into a raisin. Seth called her *ma'am*? Granted, she'd read he'd been in the military, and she was thirty-two. But his blue eyes hadn't shown even a glimmer of recognition. Had she changed that much since she was sixteen and he'd given her her first kiss?

"I hate to rush off," he said. "But I don't want to be late." His lips narrowed, as if being a little late now and then was a crime. "Let me know if I can do anything."

"I will," she said.

Seth reached down toward the baggie just as a gust of wind caught it and swirled it away, high out of reach. He watched it a second, then took a step sideways, half-turning toward the school. "C'mon, Tony. You better run by attendance and get a tardy slip."

Tony looked once more at her car, gave her an apologetic shrug, and followed him.

A second later, Pastor Corey drove up next to her. He pointed at his wrist, where someone might wear a watch, and drove out of the parking lot.

Becky pulled her phone out of her purse. Eight forty-five. Corey was on his way to the ecumenical breakfast, and she'd missed their appointment. Completely.

All to find out that the man who she'd been so excited to see didn't recognize her. Because he was too busy to even look at her.

Talk about rude.

# Chapter Two

At 8:59 a.m., Seth raced into his office. Nothing could be worse than being late for a meeting he'd requested. But he'd made it back in time, in spite of worrying about the pot in the parking lot, dealing with three kids loitering in the hall, and being distracted by that dark-haired woman whose car Tony had hit. She looked so familiar. Although he didn't have half the names straight at the high school, he knew she didn't work there. Maybe at the church.

He opened the blinds to brighten the dingy office and slid into his desk chair. Then he looked down at the seat. He could put up with the paneling on the walls and the 1970s desk, knowing the Abundance schools were short on money. But he'd ignored the smell of mildew as long as he could stand it. He had to buy a new chair. Right after he met the staff and checked on the job posting for a new secretary. Without a secretary, now that classes were back in session, this job was one notch above chaos. The only thing properly organized was the online calendar.

As if to confirm his thoughts, the phone began to ring, first one line, then the other. Seth glanced at the numbers. Both from outside the school.

He punched the button to send all calls to voice mail.

A moment later, a man knocked and poked his head in the door. "Hi. Bill Tesson, Spanish and Head Basketball Coach."

Seth gestured him in.

Bill was even taller than Seth and nearly bald. His black pants looked freshly pressed and his Abundance High polo might have seen an iron as well.

Seth shook Bill's hand and introduced himself. Of all his meetings today, this one might be the most important. If he handled it right, Bill could really help Tony.

Bill sat across the desk in a guest chair that probably also needed to be replaced. The smell of mildew had to be in that upholstery too. The coach, though, relaxed into the chair as if the odor in the principal's office didn't strike him as unusual.

Seth had looked up Bill Tesson. The coach was local, a graduate from Abundance High in the eighties, and a former Marine. Even now, he seemed highly fit and aware of his space. This was not a man who'd committed unnecessary fouls on the court or been caught unaware on a mission.

"Thanks for stopping by," Seth said. "I'm trying to say hello to everyone during their off period these first couple of days. How do your classes look this semester? And the team? Any issues?"

"No. It's all good," Bill said. "Got your email about J.W. having detention. I understand. That kid needs some boundaries."

"From what I've seen, I'd agree."

The coach crossed his arms over his chest and studied Seth. Then he bent forward, one elbow on the desk. "I've got to tell you, some folks are uncomfortable with the idea of a new principal who's an outsider. I mean, no one condones financial mismanagement, but not everyone believes it went on."

"I appreciate the warning." The situation was about what Seth had expected. Not everything had been made public yet. As more charges were filed, they'd believe. And most of the staff probably did resent him, being so young for the position and coming in from out of town. But Seth's former commanding officer, from when he'd been an instructor in the Navy, had served years ago with Roscoe and given Seth a glowing recommendation. And the superintendent wanted an outsider, had even told Seth that if things went well, he'd try to make sure the position was permanent.

"One other question, Bill," Seth said. "How do you handle things when a student moves into the district this time of year and played basketball at his former school?"

"Ah, your brother." Bill's words held a hint of disapproval and he leaned back. "I just met him in the hall near attendance, telling me he was late because of some fender bender. Kind of a mouthy kid, isn't he?"

Seth's chest tightened. "Sometimes."

Tony seemed to get along fine with that woman in the parking lot, someone he'd probably never see again. The coach, though, a person he needed to impress, he got smart with. And it was probably Seth's fault, because of what he'd said to Tony as they walked back to the school. Sometimes it seemed like the less he was around Seth, the better Tony behaved.

"I'll admit it," Seth said. "Tony needs a solid father figure, not just a brother, to help him shape up. But he's a good player, was one of the stars of the JV team back in Tennessee his freshman year. Even if he sat the bench here all year, it would be great if he could practice with the team." And Seth had asked around about the basketball program. There were drugs at the high school, but Bill had a zero-tolerance policy.

"What about his play this year?" Bill said. "If he's driving, he's got to be at least a sophomore, right?"

Seth swallowed. This was the tricky part. "Tony didn't play this year in Tennessee. He met this girl…" Did he have to spell it out, explain that, despite Seth's best efforts, his brother had given up basketball for a bleached blond with questionable morals? Explain that she'd gotten him involved with minor vandalism and pot—and with three friends who, according to what Seth had heard, were now doing things a lot worse?

"Hmm." Bill's eyes narrowed and he glanced away.

"He wants another chance to get on the court, and he's not the first guy to make a mistake because of the opposite sex."

"That's true." The coach ran one hand over his bald head. "You say he's good?"

"Scored ten to twelve points every game last year on JV. A solid rebounder, lots of hustle."

"All right. Have him come to practice tomorrow. We'll see how he does."

"Thanks, Bill. I really appreciate this."

The coach gave a dismissive wave. "Just tell him to watch his mouth. The team doesn't need a troublemaker." His phone let out a squawk, and he jolted in his seat. "Thought I had that on silent." He pulled it out, and his mouth thinned into a line as he read the text.

"Everything okay?" Seth asked.

"Not exactly. Prattsville, our big rivals, had a leak in their gym roof after that last snow. It's unstable. They can't host the boys' varsity and JV games on February fifteenth. They want to know if we can hold them here."

Seth opened the calendar on his computer. "Let me look."

"With all those makeup games because of bad weather, it will be nearly impossible to find another date that would work for both us and for Prattsville."

Seth scrolled to the next month. "That day's clear." And it wasn't a Sunday. Sunday, as Roscoe Grange had explained, had to be kept open because the school shared the parking lot with the church across the street, part of a deal worked out when the school district bought the land from the church.

Bill leaned forward. "We can hold the games here?"

"I don't see why not." He hit a few keys to enter the event on the calendar. "All booked."

Bill let out a sigh and sank back in his chair. "Excellent."

"Glad I could help." Seth rose. Time for his next meeting.

"I'll expect your brother after school tomorrow." Bill moved to the door. "Thanks for the schedule change."

Seth gave a quick wave. An excellent discussion and a great start to things here in Abundance—everyone cooperating for the good of the students.

He could set a professional tone with the teachers and staff, make a success of this interim position, and convince the school board to keep him on permanently. And Tony could spend his free time on the court—not on the streets—and graduate from high school right on schedule.

Ↄ

Becky poured creamer in her coffee, then rushed out of the church kitchen and into her tiny office to grab a notebook for her rescheduled meeting.

Corey sat in the chair across from her desk, tapping a pen against his leg. The young pastor had been with Abundance Community Church for two years, a year less than she'd had the part-time job as church pianist and director of the adult and children's choirs. Short, dark-haired, and energetic, Corey was also colorblind—which led to a few interesting shirt-and-tie combinations on Sundays. Come to think of it, today's outfit of a gray shirt and tan pants wasn't exactly *GQ*.

"Hey, Becky, I'm early, but can we talk in here?"

"Sure." She sat down. His office was more than twice the size of hers. If he could let slide the fact that she was often a couple of minutes late, usually without a solid excuse like earlier this morning, she could ignore the piles of books and papers that meant talking in his office was impossible. "How was the ecumenical breakfast?"

"Excellent. And driving back I had an idea for this week's sermon. I think you'll really like it."

"I'm sure I will." Corey might not win any awards for the tidiest office, but his sermons were almost always good. She took a sip of her coffee and smiled. The church brew tasted so much better now that she'd brought in that French vanilla creamer and stashed it in the refrigerator.

"Before I forget," Corey said, "how late are you staying today?"

The vanilla soured on her tongue. "Four thirty. I'm trying to get a lot done since I don't have to teach, but I need to drop my car at the shop by five." She tried to sound normal, as if it didn't bother her that the pastor always stuck around to lock up after she left.

It had been months since last summer's disaster. Months since she'd let everyone down. She ought to just ask him if he trusted her.

But she was afraid he'd say no.

"If you're taking your car in, you should get things checked under the hood."

She tipped her head to one side, halfway agreeing. Her Toyota had some problems starting up last summer, but after her brother Earl Ray replaced her battery, it seemed fine.

Corey leaned forward. "So what's your big idea?"

Becky set her coffee aside. "It's about the next concert for the Abundance Youth Choir."

"Okay…" He sounded as if he'd rather get back to his sermon. Which was why she wanted to meet with him. She needed his full support, now more than ever.

For almost three years, she'd been directing the town's youth choir as a volunteer, on her own time. The kids needed a chance to sing, needed to be encouraged to develop their gifts. Most churches in town, including theirs, didn't have enough kids to have individual youth choirs. Opportunities at the high school were limited and—according to the kids—often conflicted with required classes. The Abundance Youth Choir was important, and all the church provided was the space.

"Corey, the youth choir is a good outreach to kids with no church home." The practices at least got kids from all over town in the church doors, even if it wasn't for worship.

He raised one eyebrow as if not completely sold.

"I know we haven't seen results yet, and I know one member of the church council thinks I should spend that time helping her daughter work on a children's choir solo. But that little girl doesn't want to do a solo. And even if only one youth choir member feels comfortable enough to visit our church and hear how much God loves them, it will be worth it. Plus the idea I had last night will make the next concert even better."

Corey raised his head, as if she might have caught his attention. "Go on."

"The volunteers at the food pantry are worried that supplies are really low this winter. I can't stand to think of them possibly running out." Especially not since she'd been volunteering there. Once she met the people the

24

pantry served, the ministry seemed more important. She'd even seen the mother of one of her youth choir members there after the woman lost her job. Becky scooted forward in her chair. "We could ask everyone who comes to the concert to bring a couple of canned goods to donate."

"Oh, I like that idea, really like it."

Excitement filled Becky's chest like helium in a balloon, and a smile stretched across her face.

"I think you'd get a lot of donations. Maybe even enough to last the winter."

"I hope so." She couldn't bear to think of people going hungry. "And you know that job I'm applying for, the one you wrote a reference for?"

"Yes."

"I realized this morning that a successful concert benefiting the food pantry might even help my chances."

"I can see that," he said. "Especially if people see how well you've developed the choir's talent."

Not exactly what she meant. Her qualifications as a music teacher were solid. She was afraid people didn't trust her anymore, didn't think she cared about the community. A benefit concert would prove her commitment to the town.

"Sounds good." Corey stood. "I better go call the church consultant back and get his visit set up."

"Corey?" Midge stuck her head in the doorway. "A woman's in the main office, wanting to speak to the minister. I texted like you asked, but..."

Corey pulled out his phone. "Sorry. I didn't even hear it." He turned back to Becky. "Keep me posted."

"Will do." Becky gave the church office manager her friendliest smile. "How's your day going, Midge?"

"Fine." Somehow, though, in one word, the woman implied that the day had been better before she'd seen Becky.

Becky slid down in her chair, her balloon of excitement popped. Another attempt, another rejection.

She and Midge had never been close. Normally Becky only worked at the church a few hours a week. Midge was older, quiet, and sort of hard to read. But since last summer, even though Becky had repeatedly apologized for her part in the scandal, even though Midge said she'd forgiven her, there had been a distinct chill in their interactions.

Which posed a problem.

Midge's husband was the school superintendent.

How was Becky supposed to get a fair shot at the position teaching music in the Abundance elementary schools? If Midge was against her, she didn't have a chance.

❦

"J.W. and Johnny, you can sit there and there." Seth pointed to two chairs on opposite sides of his outer office, where—he'd learned earlier in the afternoon—he wouldn't have a secretary for three weeks. "Do your homework. Hands to yourself. Mouths shut." Firm, clear directions, exactly like the ones he'd given the student body at the assembly during third period.

And just as well received. Johnny sank down, head lowered. J.W. gave Seth an angry glare.

Seth ignored them both, went into his inner office, and shut the glass door to block out the noise of the students in the hallway. Too bad he couldn't block the mildew smell too.

Sadly, any trips to shop for new furniture in Columbia would have to wait. Between the end of lunch, when he'd supervised all 300 students in the cafeteria, and 3:30 p.m., when the last bell rang, he'd talked with the local cops about the drugs in the high school and met with eight teachers, as well as one very disgruntled aide.

What a day. At least he'd had a good conversation with the basketball coach. He couldn't wait to tell Tony the news.

He turned on his computer and started an email to the superintendent, updating him on the meeting with the police. The drug situation here wasn't good, but it was better than it had been in Tennessee.

"Hey, I got your text." Tony leaned against the inner doorway, a loaded backpack slung over one shoulder. "You wanted me to stop by before I drove home?"

Seth waved him inside and gestured for him to shut the door and take a seat. That full backpack was a good sign.

Tony slid down in the chair across the desk.

Seth looked him in the eye. "The pot in the parking lot?"

Tony jerked upright. "Not mine."

Seth stared at him a moment, then waved for him to relax. "I had to check, but I didn't really think it was." Partly because Tony seemed like he was trying. Partly because the kid had never been stupid enough to leave any hint of his drug use lying around. "And that's not what I asked you here for."

"Then what?" Tony sat back down and glanced around the room. "Seth, this office stinks."

"I know." Seth and his brother butted heads three times a day lately, but they both had the Williams' strong sense of smell. "The upholstery's mildewed."

Tony looked down at his chair and wrinkled his nose.

"These chairs must be twenty years old. I need to get to an office supply store in Columbia and buy a couple of new ones. How about we go Saturday and eat some seafood while we're down there?"

"Shrimp?" Tony's eyes lit like they had when he'd first come to live with Seth four years ago and been delighted to go out for seafood.

"Shrimp," Seth said, suddenly a little nostalgic for the time when—after the first rough months with Tony—he'd thought parenting was mostly logistics and laundry. Back then Tony had been glad just to have a responsible adult who cared.

Seth still harbored remnants of guilt over the fact that he had been the lucky brother. After the divorce, when Dad left Mom and him and later married Tony's mother, Mom had done her best to give Seth a good home. Years later, after Tony's mother died when he was twelve, Dad hadn't done nearly as well as a single parent.

Tony wound up in Social Services.

Even though Seth had only met Tony a few times back then, he'd felt he should step up and be there for his half-brother. The kid didn't have any other family. Now Seth needed to stand by his commitments, be the parent his dad had never been, and get Tony through high school.

If a platter of shrimp would help, Seth was more than happy to buy it. "We'll do it. Seafood. Saturday lunch. And I talked to the basketball coach. That's why I called you in. You can go to practice tomorrow. He might even let you on the JV team if you look good. If"—he bent forward, elbows on the desk—"you lose the attitude. Coach Tesson is the guy you saw outside the attendance office."

"That guy is a jerk. Like a lot of people in this dinky little town."

Heat built in Seth's chest. "The coach is not a jerk. You two just got off on the wrong foot. And we talked about this. Being on the team here is exactly what you need to make friends and get your life on track."

"When are you going to understand?" Tony lurched to his feet. "It's my life. You're not in charge of me."

"I am in charge." Seth struggled to keep his temper in check. "For two more years. It's a good thing too. You still need to learn some manners. And you need to learn to pay attention. Like when you're driving."

Tony's chin jutted out. "I *was* paying attention. I hit some ice in the parking lot. You didn't even let me explain."

Seth's stomach sank and he sat back in his chair. "Ice?" He hadn't taught Tony how to drive on ice. Back in Tennessee they hadn't even had any bad weather this year.

"Yeah, ice." Fear crept into Tony's voice. "The car just slid." He cleared his throat and went on, his tone angry. "But *you* think everything is my fault."

"I...I thought the roads and parking lot were all clear," Seth said. He should be telling his brother that fitting into a new town took time. Instead, once again he'd been too rigid, too critical, and fallen short at parenting. He tried so hard to do better than his dad, but... "We'll go out next time it snows and practice. And I'll tell the school maintenance crew, so they can put out more salt."

Tony's jaw relaxed and he leaned against a filing cabinet. "Next time, give me the benefit of the doubt, will you?"

"I will. As long as you give basketball another try."

"All right. I still think that coach is a jerk. But I know I messed up in Tennessee. I'm trying to do better. Even if you don't notice it, I am paying attention."

"Fair enough. You go to practice tomorrow, and Saturday we'll eat mountains of shrimp." He walked around the desk and clapped Tony on the shoulder.

Tony gave him a lopsided grin.

"Be careful out there." Seth gestured over his shoulder to the window.

"I will. That ice is probably melted by now. It got pretty warm."

"I'll be home in a couple of hours. Can you throw that frozen lasagna in the oven?"

"Sure." Tony's eyes gleamed. "You know, I could eat half of one of those." He tossed his backpack over his shoulder and headed toward the hall.

Seth ran a hand over his forehead. Yeah, Tony could eat half of one of those lasagnas. The size that was supposed to serve twelve. But he'd said he'd give basketball a try. Once he was on the court, everything would fall into place.

For now, Seth needed to call his insurance company. He'd meant to do it hours ago.

He found his insurance card and pulled out the paper Tony had given him, then noticed the name of the woman in the parking lot.

Becky Hamlin.

*Becky Hamlin?*

A hollow tingling spread through his chest. No wonder she seemed familiar. If only he'd looked at her eyes. If only…

…he'd been paying attention.

# Chapter Three

Becky set two glasses of water on her hand-me-down kitchen table and collapsed onto a chair beside it.

Her cousin Abby flopped down in the chair across from her and gestured to the living room. "I think you planned that."

"Nope." Becky took a long drink of water.

"You call me at my antique shop just before closing to tell me you've bought paint and want to show me the colors and right when I stop by, you're moving the piano?" Abby pushed back a few strands of light-brown hair that had escaped her ponytail.

"That was just luck. I had no idea you'd stop by today. But I do appreciate the help."

Abby rolled her eyes. "I wanted to see if you were okay after the wreck this morning."

"I'm fine. It was just a fender bender."

"And I wanted to see the colors," Abby said. "I think I'm more excited about this project than you are."

"That's because you won't be doing the painting."

"I'm a little busy in the evenings." Abby glanced toward her daughter, Emma, who stood by the stove, watching Becky's cat.

Twizzler—black as licorice except for one white paw—wound himself around Emma's ankles and purred at top volume.

Abby turned back to Becky, her face suddenly more serious. "Hey, speaking of Emma, about Thursday—?"

"I'm looking forward to it."

Two-year-old Emma was a sweetheart and such a cutie. Her reddish-gold curls had been inherited from her father, but her wide smile resembled her mother's.

Abby's eyebrows drew together. "But my mom said you won great tickets to some big concert in Columbia."

"And I already have plans to give them to one of my choir members." Becky was going to tell Katiana Marcum's mom that she couldn't go and offer her and her daughter the seats. After she'd seen Mrs. Marcum at the food pantry, it seemed like the perfect idea. Katiana had been talking about how much she wanted to see the concert.

"But you shouldn't give up the tickets just to babysit for me when my folks are busy. I could ask someone else."

"It's not a big deal. I can go to a concert any time. You almost never get a break from mom duties, and I'm not having you miss your photography class. Besides, Emma and I always have fun when I watch her."

"But—"

"I'm not listening. No way are you depriving me of time with my favorite little girl."

Abby frowned. "All right. I guess," she said slowly. "I have already missed one class when she was sick."

"I talked to Corey today," Becky said before Abby could change her mind. "He likes the idea of the canned goods drive. Thinks it could really help the local food pantry."

"Good. I hope it does. A benefit like that could do a lot to improve your reputation around town and might even help you get the job you want."

"Or at least a fair shot at it." She'd love to teach in Abundance. "The pay's a lot better than the Wellsby Academy, and there'd be more potential for job security. You never quite know with a private school."

"Plus I worry about you commuting when the roads are icy."

"It has been scary a time or two." And that hour drive to Columbia could take a lot longer in bad weather.

Yet a measure of guilt still troubled her over the idea that she was using the event for her own advantage. When Becky had first thought of making the concert a benefit, it was strictly to make amends to the food pantry. Did the fact that she'd realized it might also help her professionally mean she was doing the benefit for the wrong reason? She hoped not, as long as she was upfront about it.

"With no commute time, it would make it easier to do your choir work during business hours," Abby said.

"You know, so you could have more time to meet with Corey…and discuss church things."

Meeting with Corey wasn't difficult. He was usually around. And choir practices had to be in the evenings. Becky shrugged and took another drink of water. "The job's still a long shot. Some people still blame me for letting that money get stolen last summer. So feel free to tell folks that I hope the concert makes things up to the food pantry, but please keep my application a secret. I don't want people to know that I applied if I don't get it."

"Okay, I promise." Abby held up three fingers in a Brownie salute. "I won't mention it to anyone but God."

"He's already heard all about it from me. I've been praying about this job for weeks."

"Then you need to have faith." Abby nodded her head emphatically. "I think you've got a great chance. I heard that after Mrs. Martin died, the school had a terrible time finding a qualified long-term sub, and the one they found is moving out of the area come June. That's why they started the search for the permanent position so early. And the benefit concert idea is brilliant. You could even collect cash donations at the door. I'm pretty sure the pantry has ways to buy more food with a dollar than you and I can."

Becky shrank back in her chair. She was nervous enough already. What if the canned goods collection was low, simply because of her? "Uh, I think I should let some other group collect cash."

Abby leaned in. "Do people still act like they don't trust you? Besides Midge?"

Becky's stomach twisted, and she looked at the linoleum. She couldn't mention Corey. It was too awful to say out loud that their own pastor didn't trust her. "Some of them."

"Well, some people are idiots. The school would be lucky to get you. I don't know a single teacher who cares about her students as much as you do." She glanced at the wall calendar, a freebie from the bank. "When's the concert again?"

"Friday, February fifteenth."

"Friday?" Abby's brow crinkled. "What about parking? I thought the school almost always had something on Fridays."

"Already taken care of. I talked with Yvonne before all that trouble started at the high school and had her block off the Friday of Presidents' Day weekend on their master calendar. I wanted the concert then because we're doing all patriotic music."

"Fabulous." Abby scooped her daughter onto her lap. "See, Emma? Everything is going to work out great."

ඏ

After dinner that night, Seth climbed out of his SUV and looked at the little white house. He checked the address Becky had given with her insurance information. Yep, this was her place. In the summer, the one-and-a-half-story bungalow outside Abundance was probably quiet and peaceful, its porch swing a perfect spot to relax. Now, mid-winter, with wind that felt like it was blowing in from the Arctic instead of Kansas, the house seemed isolated and lonely.

Kind of how Seth felt, being new in town.

And the one person who might be a friend, who might help him make a good impression on the town, he hadn't even recognized.

Of course, he hadn't been expecting to see Becky. It had been a long time since he was fifteen. And he hadn't known to look for her when he moved to Abundance. The church camp where they'd met all those years ago had served the whole state, and Seth had grown up hours away, down in Springfield. He did sort of remember her saying she was from north of Columbia, though. Maybe this was her hometown.

Whatever the case, he needed to make amends, not simply for old times' sake, but because part of his job was to maintain good relations with the community. And he'd like to find a way for Tony to take some responsibility for hitting her car. Her driveway was gravel, but maybe his brother could shovel her sidewalk a few times over the winter.

He climbed onto the front porch, heard the earthy tones of jazz inside, and knocked on the bright turquoise door.

After a few seconds the music stopped, cutting off a saxophone solo.

Becky opened the door. Her dark hair was pulled back in a ponytail, and she held a paint roller with beige paint on it. She stiffened, and her eyes looked guarded. "Hello."

Deep in Seth's chest, something stirred like bubbles rising through warm syrup. He took a half-step back and stared. How could he *not* have recognized her? The shape of her face, those huge brown eyes, those long lashes—they were still the same as all those years ago at camp. "Hey, Becky. I wanted to apologize for earlier. You seemed familiar, but I couldn't figure it out until I saw your name on the insurance information. I think my brain is overloaded with being interim principal."

"It's no big deal," she said, but her tone hinted that it might have been.

Huge, icy drops of rain began to fall, and the wind picked up. Even under the cover of Becky's wide front porch, he could feel the rain hitting his back.

"Please, come in. Let me, uh…" She backed away and put the roller in a tray.

He stepped inside, and the smell of paint and a home-cooked dinner—maybe vegetable soup—surrounded him. The living room carpet was covered in plastic, the baseboards lined with blue masking tape. Furniture, including a piano and a bright red couch, had been shoved in the middle of the room and tented in plastic. One wall, freshly painted, was bright turquoise like the front door.

"Sorry. I wasn't expecting company." Becky tugged at the hem of her pink T-shirt as if trying to pull it over the hips of her yoga pants.

Time to smooth things over. "I don't mean to interrupt. This room is going to look great, though." The turquoise wall and red couch were way too much color for his taste, but he tried to sound convincing.

"Thank you," she said, but her eyes looked skeptical. "I'd ask you to sit down, but as you can see, my living room is out of commission." She swiped at her face, smearing beige paint across one cheek.

He was making her uncomfortable. His attempt at community relations was failing. He needed to fix this. That principal's job was too important and—

His stomach tightened. Becky had been a sweetheart at sixteen, and all he was worried about was his job. He should be thinking about things from her perspective. He pulled out his keys and held them toward her in his open palm. "I wanted to apologize again for Tony's hitting your car. If your car has to go in the shop, I'd be happy to let you drive mine for a few days if you need it. Tony and I could share his truck."

Her face softened. "Oh, thanks, but the repair place gave me a loaner."

"Okay. I would like my brother to do something to make up for hitting your car, though. How about a few hours of help painting tomorrow night?"

"That's not necessary."

"Even though he skidded on a patch of ice, I'd like him to take some responsibility."

Becky angled her head to one side, then nodded as if she approved of his quasi-parenting skills. She looked at the walls, then at the tiny patch of beige she had finished. "All right. Any time after five. I'll be painting for hours. I have to do the hall and kitchen too. There's no trim between the rooms."

"I think he can be here by seven."

"Wonderful." She took a half-step toward him. "Hey, where have you been going to church since you moved to town?"

Seth edged back. "Um, I hadn't really…"

"You've probably been super busy. I'm the choir director at Abundance Community Church. You should give us a try."

"Thanks. I'll keep that in mind." He zipped his coat a little higher. Not an invitation he planned to take her up on, but still, he needed to be polite. "Well, I don't mean to hold you up. I just wanted to say I was sorry I didn't recognize you. It might have been the glasses."

"Oh," she said slowly. She touched the fingers of one hand to her temple, as if reaching for missing glasses. "I got contacts."

"It's a good look."

"Thanks." There'd been a tension in her eyes before, but it eased, and she looked even more like the girl he remembered. A shy smile teased the corners of her lips, and that syrupy feeling melted through his heart like it had when she'd come to the door.

"I hope you like living here in Abundance." Her tone was warm now, as if she really meant it.

"I think I will." He gazed at her brown eyes once more, then opened the door. "I'll send Tony over tomorrow." Halfway down her sidewalk, despite the wind and rain, he looked back. He'd made definite progress in community relations.

And found that living in Abundance held all kinds of attractions he hadn't expected.

# Chapter Four

The next evening Becky squeezed out of her spare room and closed the door before Twizzler could escape.

He let out an angry *mmrrooww*.

She'd taken a break from painting and gone in to pet him, but he'd twitched his tail and jerked his head away from her. She'd never go so far as to say Twizzler pouted, but he was quite skilled at communicating when she failed to meet his expectations. Like now, a triple-demerit day. The store had been out of his favorite cat-food flavor, fish and shrimp. She'd served beef-and-liver flavor, a sorry substitute. She'd committed a further offense by bringing stinky paint into the house. And like yesterday, she'd imprisoned him.

But she couldn't risk him getting into wet paint. "Take a nap, sweetie," she called through the door. "Or play with your new catnip mouse." A fifty-fifty chance there. Sometimes Twizzler loved them. Sometimes he rejected them.

For a moment, she admired the hallway she'd painted last night. Town Taupe was a good color, warm but not too orange. She refilled her tray, started on the edge work in the living room, and listened for a car in the driveway. She'd ask Tony to do the high part of the living room walls. Tall as he was, he might not even need the ladder.

Maybe Seth would drop him off and come in to say hello. She certainly wouldn't complain if he did. Unlike yesterday, when he'd looked so handsome and she'd been wearing those ancient yoga pants that made her hips look big, today she had on leggings and a long red T-shirt. Both old and appropriate for painting, but much more flattering.

She also wouldn't complain if he started attending Abundance Community Church. Pretty much, she'd welcome any chance to see him.

The doorbell rang.

Becky laid her brush across the tray and got to her feet, careful not to pull the plastic away from the baseboard, then opened the door.

Tony stood on the porch, alone, hair wet, hands in his front pockets. "Hi."

"Thank you so much for coming over to help me. Let me take your coat."

He shrugged it off his shoulders, and she laid it on a chair in the kitchen. No Seth. She pushed back her disappointment. Maybe she could learn a bit from Tony, though, like why Seth was still single. After all, if he was married, the article in the local paper would have mentioned his wife. She'd read the *Abundance News* enough years to know.

Tony walked toward the painting supplies, then stopped as if he'd remembered something. "I'm really sorry I hit your car, Miss Hamlin. Katiana, this girl in my history class, says you're awfully nice, that you're the only adult in the whole town that knows how to listen."

"Katiana Marcum?"

"Yeah." A hint of pink crept up his throat.

"She's a very sweet girl." And cute, but it seemed Tony had already noticed.

Katiana was also a promising soprano, which Tony probably didn't know. Might not even care if he did.

Becky didn't like to assume, but most people didn't have much appreciation for the fine arts. All they cared about these days was sports. Well, not just these days. Back when she'd been in high school, everyone had been so impressed that both her brothers had made all-state football. No one cared that she'd made all-state choir.

But she ought to let that go and focus on painting.

She stepped closer to Tony. "So, how high can you reach without a ladder?"

"In here?" He looked up. "The whole wall."

"Perfect. Have you painted before?"

"Seth and I did most of the rooms in the house back in Tennessee before it went on the market."

She handed him a brush. "Great. Why don't you start on the edging near the top?"

"Sure thing."

Within ten minutes, she could see that what Tony lacked in driving skills he more than made up for in painting. The boy was fast, got good coverage, and painted right up to the ceiling but not on it. "I can't tell you how much I appreciate this," she said. "I bet we can finish the first coat in the living room in a couple of hours. I'll have to tell your brother what wonderful help you are."

"Thanks." Tony loaded more paint onto his brush. "I didn't realize yesterday morning that you already knew him."

"Well, it was a long time ago. We were about your age when we went to the same church camp. I would have figured he had a wife and three kids by now."

"Nope, no wife. And just me for a kid. I'm probably the reason he's single. I mean, I know I take a lot of his time. Until a couple of months ago, he had to drive me everywhere and—"

"I'm sure Seth is very happy to have you in his life," Becky said quickly. She hadn't thought about what it must be like for Seth to take care of his brother. And certainly hadn't meant to make Tony feel bad about it.

But Tony's shoulders had lifted at her later comment. He clearly wanted Seth to like him, probably more than Seth knew. Teenagers were funny. One minute so mature, the next like little kids.

"From the way he told me six times to be polite, I got the impression he was pretty happy to have you in his life too." Tony winked.

Becky's cheeks grew warm. There. The perfect example. He was acting way too mature. She glanced away. She'd thought she could ask a few subtle questions, learn about Seth's past. This kid would see right through her.

Still, she liked what Tony said. Not something she really wanted him to notice, though, but he wasn't likely to. He'd now plugged earbuds into his phone and was listening to something while he painted.

She got back to work as well.

Five minutes later, though, she stopped—and listened. Absorbed in his work, Tony had started singing along to his music. And he was good.

She waved at him and motioned for him to take out his earbuds. "You've got a great voice. I'm the director of the Abundance Youth Choir. You should think about joining."

He shook his head. "I wouldn't have time with basketball."

"You'd get to see Katiana," she said, unable to resist.

He raised both eyebrows in an expression that said he didn't need her help with his love life. "Not happening. Seth wants me on the court. The more hours in practice, the better."

"Does he want you to try for an athletic scholarship?"

"Nah," Tony said with a laugh. "I'm not that good. Seth…"

She angled her head closer. *Seth what?*

"He thinks if I spend a lot of time in practice, if I get the discipline, I won't end up like our dad did. You know, in prison."

Becky almost dropped her brush. She struggled to act like the tidbit was old news. But it wasn't. And it wasn't what she'd expected to learn from Tony about Seth. Not by a long shot.

♋

Sunday morning, Becky stood behind the last row of pews in the sanctuary and scanned the room. She'd invited Seth to church, she'd invited her youth choir—as she did every week—and she'd invited a husband and wife who were new to town that she met when she was buying paint. If any of them were here, she wanted to say hi before she went to the choir room.

Outside, sunlight bounced off the snow and filtered through the huge windows. Each windowsill held a tall, thick white candle and evergreen boughs that made the church still smell like Christmas. The early arrivals and the people coming in from Sunday school, like her family, had already staked out their favorite pews.

Her sister-in-law, Stacey, sat next to Mom and Dad. One row behind them, her friend Tess sat with her husband, Becky's cousin Jack. From upstairs came laughter that was almost certainly from her brother Earl Ray, about to run the sound booth.

There were lots of other people she knew, but none of the visitors she was looking for.

Abby walked up beside her. "Hey, why so glum?"

"Oh, sorry, I didn't mean to look sad. I was just checking to see if anyone I'd invited was here today."

"No such luck?"

"No." Not even Seth.

"Well, I think it's nice that you invite people. You're so good about that. Maybe they'll come in later." Abby gave her an encouraging smile. "Hopefully, if they do, they won't hold Pastor Corey's fashion sense against us. Did you see his shirt and tie this morning?"

"No." But it didn't take much to imagine that the combination was probably another doozy.

"Not pretty. That man needs a wife."

Becky chuckled. She knew for a fact that Corey had a secret fear that someone in the congregation would sign him up for an internet dating site. "I'd better go get the music out. I'll see you in the choir room in five minutes."

Abby waved and walked away.

Becky stopped to say hi to her family, got the music folders out of the closet, and helped the choir members warm up. She followed them into the sanctuary, then sat down at the piano and glanced out into the pews. Still no youth choir members, no couple from the paint store, no Seth.

Across from her, Corey cleared his throat.

Time to focus on worship. She began the prelude.

A few minutes later, when she'd finished playing the first hymn, she glanced out again. Katiana Marcum was sliding into one of the pews with her mother.

Becky beamed at the girl. Katiana didn't attend church elsewhere, and she'd never come to Abundance Community before. The youth choir must have played a part. But it would be wrong to interrupt Corey while he was welcoming visitors, just so she could point that out.

Becky began the next hymn and made a renewed effort to keep her mind on worship. After she finished the fourth verse, she moved to a chair behind the piano, and

Corey began the sermon. She glanced back at the congregation.

Katiana seemed to be listening attentively to Corey talk about turning the pain of one's past over to God. What with checking on her and looking again for Seth, Becky didn't quite catch all of the message, but the congregation seemed really engaged, as if the sermon was one of Corey's best. She'd have to remember to tell him.

And invite Seth again, maybe mention what a good preacher Corey was.

At the end of the service, she slid off the piano bench, eager to talk to Katiana. But two of her older choir members, deep in a conversation about someone in the hospital, blocked her exit from the piano area.

Luckily, Katiana was walking right toward her.

Becky leaned over the railing. "I'm so glad you and your mom came to visit our church today."

"Thanks for inviting us. We both really liked it. We've thought about coming before, but Mom's been pretty down. Not anymore, though. She just got a new job as a custodian at the hospital."

"That's wonderful! Tell her congratulations. And I'm glad you liked the service."

Katiana toyed with the ends of her blonde hair and worried her lower lip. "Um, Mom said now that she's working again, I should ask you about the time you've been helping me after choir practice. Should we be paying you for private lessons?"

"No." Becky waved one hand dismissively. "That's just part of being choir director."

Katiana's face brightened.

"And if we ever do official voice lessons," Becky said, "we could always work something out. Like maybe you could help me weed my garden this summer." She did have a few private voice and piano students. The money was good. But she always offered another way. Everyone who loved music deserved encouraging.

"Thank you. And thanks again for those tickets." Katiana waved. "See you at practice."

"See you. Glad you came to church."

Katiana turned to leave, then spun back around. "I almost forgot. Doesn't our concert conflict with the home game?"

Becky picked up the hymnal from the music rack of the piano. "There's no home game that night. I talked with Yvonne about parking months ago. She put our concert on the high school schedule."

"Maybe with all those problems it got changed? Because I saw it online. It says in all caps, 'ABUNDANCE VS. PRATTSVILLE, FEBRUARY 15, GAME MOVED TO HOME.'"

Becky's chest went numb. Her hymnal crashed onto the keyboard with a discordant bang.

Members of the congregation stopped chatting in the aisles and turned toward the piano.

She gave them a quick, nervous wave and a nothing's-wrong smile.

Which was a total lie. Something was definitely wrong. Prattsville was Abundance High School's biggest rival and less than half an hour away. If there was a home basketball game against the Prattsville Raiders the night of her concert, parking would be impossible.

# Chapter Five

Seth straightened the pile of papers on his lap and put them on the floor beside his recliner. Done. At last he felt ready for the week ahead. He and Tony had found two new chairs for his office yesterday, and he'd just put in a good solid Sunday morning of work— exactly what he needed to make sure this interim principal position became permanent.

He'd even taken a break and made pancakes for brunch, much to his brother's delight.

Tony, who might possibly still be full an hour after he'd eaten eight pancakes, lay on the couch, flipping through channels on the TV.

"Hey," Seth said. "It's almost time for pre-ga—" His phone rang and he grabbed it off the end table.

Wasn't the number the same one he'd given his insurance agent? Becky's.

His pulse sped as he hit Talk.

"Seth? It's Becky Hamlin." Her voice sounded higher than normal, and her words were rushed.

"Is everything okay?"

"No. There's been some mix-up. I'm planning a community youth concert at the church, and I learned there's a high school home basketball game that night."

"When?"

"February fifteenth."

"Oh." There hadn't been any concert on the calendar that night. Seth got up and went into the kitchen. "The other school had a leak in their gym. It wouldn't be safe to have the game there."

"But that's the night of my concert."

He leaned back against the counter. Why had she scheduled her concert for a Friday? The parking lot was reserved for the church on Sundays. "Um, how about we grab a cup of coffee at Cassidy's Diner and figure this out?"

"Thank you. It's going to be hard to get a table, though. Half the congregation is probably still there."

"Not a problem. I'll go on over and wait for a table. Can you meet me there in twenty minutes?"

"Okay. I have to talk to someone first, but I can be there at one."

ଔ

Fifteen minutes later, Seth slid into a slick vinyl booth at the diner and glanced around the room. Becky had been right. The place was packed. And smelled amazing, like onions fried in butter and those cinnamon rolls he'd heard about. Maybe he'd get a couple to take home so he and Tony could have them for breakfast.

One o'clock came and went.

He finished his coffee and looked at email on his phone. Becky must have gotten held up. Not a big deal. Besides, he was trying to be less rigid. She was only seven—no eight—minutes late.

At ten after one, Becky rushed in, scooted into the booth across from him, and took off her coat, revealing a cream-colored dress. "Sorry I'm late," she whispered. "I ran into a parent who wouldn't stop talking about how her tone-deaf daughter would do a great job with a solo in the children's choir." Becky pressed her lips together and gave a slight shake of her head.

"Sounds awkward." And really, something she couldn't have rushed. All the more reason for him to be flexible.

"Yeah. Her daughter's adorable, but she doesn't even want a solo. Just Mom does." Becky folded her coat and put it on the seat beside her.

"Did you get lunch?"

"I had a meeting after church and brought a sandwich. You?"

"Big brunch." Uh-oh. Now she was probably going to ask why he didn't take her up on her invitation to church. Not something he wanted to discuss. "Tell me about the concert."

"I'm so glad you're the principal," she said. "That game will need to be changed to another day. It's going to be a great concert, and we're combining it with a canned goods drive to benefit the food pantry that serves Abundance and Prattsville."

The waitress appeared, refilled his coffee, and took Becky's drink order.

Seth took a sip. How to word this? He wanted to be flexible and help, but he could only go so far. "I'm sorry, Becky, but I don't see how we can move that ball game." With no record of the concert, how could he justify the change to the administration or to Bill Tesson and the team, or even to Prattsville?

"But what about our concert?" she said, her voice indignant.

Seth picked up the salt shaker and passed it back and forth between his hands. This was the sort of situation where he tended to come off as rigid. But he was working on that. And he didn't want to be at odds with her. Quite the opposite. If he could give a little, and she could give a little, maybe they could find a solution. He set the salt down. "How bad would it be to run the two events at the same time?"

"You haven't driven around the neighborhood much, have you?" Her tone made it clear that she wasn't on board with the Let's-Both-Be-Flexible plan.

"No." He went straight to work and then home. No secretary, starting mid-year after three people had been fired, trying to keep an eye on Tony—he didn't have time for touring Abundance.

"The area around the school has lots of apartments and smaller houses with no garages. Everyone parks on the street. That's why the school and the church have the agreement."

"I've read the agreement. It doesn't say anything about the church using the parking lot on Friday nights. The church gets the lot on Sundays."

Becky's lips grew thin. "I know, but it's not set in concrete. Like when the school wants to have a Sunday matinee for a play. And a few times a year, as long as we talked with Yvonne, the former principal's secretary, they let us have the parking lot on a day other than Sunday."

"I can see how there could be some flexibility." Like how the school needed the church to be accommodating. "But—"

"I talked with Yvonne." Becky's voice grew tenser. "She promised she'd block off the night on the calendar. Read the date back to me and everything."

"Becky," he said, slowing down in the hopes that she might start to understand, "there's no record of your concert on the calendar." The home game had even been publicized. If she'd talked to him earlier... "What if the concert was Friday afternoon?"

"While the kids have school and their parents are at work?"

Okay, so that wasn't the answer. She didn't need to sound quite so annoyed though. "How about that Sunday night? Or Saturday night?" He pulled out his phone and opened the school's website.

"Sunday night won't work. That's when our church has youth group. I can't compete with that. But I guess we could hold the concert Saturday the sixteenth." Her face brightened and she leaned forward.

He wouldn't have thought it possible, but in that second, she looked even more beautiful than before. "Let me see." He checked the calendar, and his heart sank. "No, the whole day of the sixteenth is booked. Wow. Every day is booked."

She scooted back, shoulders slumped. "So much for the concert."

"I'm sorry, Becky. There was nothing on the calendar when the coach came to me on Monday."

"Came to *you*? I thought the mix-up must have happened weeks ago and I just learned about it. But you approved the game? On Monday?" Her eyes widened and her voice hit a shrill note.

His mouth went dry.

The waitress set down Becky's drink and backed away.

Seth took a sip of coffee, then steepled his hands in front of him. "February fifteenth was completely empty, and I was told the calendar was accurate."

Becky crossed her arms over her chest and blew out an angry breath. "I still think the school needs to honor its commitment."

Frankly Seth was more concerned about the commitment he'd made. Even so, the coffee hit his stomach as if it had been laced with bleach. There had to be some answer. "You said it's a choir for the whole town, right? What if the concert was held somewhere else? Maybe at another church?"

"I guess." She dragged out her words. "If that's my only option. There's only one other place in town that's big enough. St. Paul's."

"Do any of your choir members attend there?"

"Four of them. I guess I can ask." Her forehead creased as if she was considering it. She painstakingly tore off her straw wrapper and rolled it into a tight cylinder.

"If the concerts are usually at your church, it might be good to hold one at another church. Make it more of a community event."

After a moment, she tilted her head and gave a sideways nod. "Maybe you're right." She sipped her iced tea.

At last. He'd known they could find a professional solution. A sense of ease flowed through him, and he beamed at her.

She smiled back.

It wasn't a whole-hearted smile—wasn't the smile he really wanted—but it was a start.

"Anyway," she said. "Thanks for sending Tony over the other night. He was a ton of help painting."

"I appreciate you telling me. He'd gotten in with a bad crowd back in Tennessee, but he's a good kid underneath."

She drank more tea, then picked up her coat. "Hey. I'm baby-sitting my nephew this afternoon so I can't stay, but I always wondered something." She leaned closer. "How come you never came back to camp?"

"Oh." He slid his coffee cup in front of him and held it in both hands. "My parents got divorced. Dad never paid any child support. Mom didn't have the money to send me and didn't want to take charity."

"I tried to email you, but I must have gotten the address wrong. And I looked for you that next summer," Becky said. Her words grew softer. "I missed you."

Warmth spread through his chest. "I missed you too," he said in a low voice. He ought to tell her that he'd received the email, printed it out, and carried it in his wallet. Instead he reached for the check. "I'll get this. And…how about I take you out to dinner tonight? To make up for the mix-up with the calendar? I mean, if you're not seeing anyone."

A smile bloomed on her face, and the corners of her eyes crinkled. "I'm not seeing anyone." She stood up and slid on her coat. "And I'd love that."

"Great," he said. "I'll pick you up at six."

"Perfect."

෮

Seth turned onto Becky's long driveway that evening and drove toward her house. Ever since she'd said she missed him at camp, he'd alternated between good sense, with his feet firmly on the ground, and feeling like a kid in a bouncy house.

Half of him, the logical half, knew nothing could ever come of a date with Becky Hamlin. She worked in a church, and he'd wised up quite a bit since they attended youth camp together, realized that organized religion was a farce. He also knew that disparity wasn't the basis of a good relationship. Logic said he should discretely hide the flowers he'd brought in the trunk before he walked up to the house. Without them, he could play the whole evening cool, a simple gesture to make up for all the bother the ball game was causing her.

But part of him, a corner of his heart that must have been saved for Becky since he was fifteen, said religion was irrelevant and that this was *the* date, *the* girl he was meant to be with, and he'd better not blow it.

He parked and turned off the engine. A floodlight illuminated her front yard, and here and there a snowflake floated down from the clouds that blocked the moon.

He picked up the bouquet and ran one fingertip across the velvety petal of a daisy. His mind slid back a decade and a half, to a day at camp.

That day, just as he'd hoped, he'd found Becky alone. He'd seen her best friend on the path from the lake, rushing to the main lodge to take a phone call, and learned she left Becky to put away a canoe. So he gathered a huge handful of daisies from the field and sprinted to the boathouse.

He stepped inside, and as his eyes adjusted to the gloom, he saw her putting the paddles back on the rack.

"Hey." He hesitated, flowers behind his back. She was a year older, a year that suddenly gaped between them like a chasm.

She looked toward him. "Hey." Her glasses were spotted with water, her hair hung in two drippy braids, and her T-shirt and shorts were soaked. "I fell in." She gave him a small, embarrassed smile.

He walked toward her. "I've done that," he said quickly. Except he wasn't really sure he had. His brain seemed to have shorted out. "I—" He held out the flowers.

Her cheeks turned the softest pink, and her smile spread, sweet and warm and encouraging. She took the flowers and held them in both hands in front of her.

His heart pounded so hard that it echoed in his head. "Becky, I...I really like you," he mumbled. More than anything, he wanted to kiss her. But he'd never kissed a girl. And now the stupid flowers were in the way.

"I really like you too," she whispered. She took a step closer and shifted the flowers to one hand, to the side.

The air in the boathouse grew warmer, and his heart beat faster.

He laid his hand lightly on her arm and brought his lips to hers. Electricity surged through his veins.

Then the waterfront director barged in. Seth leapt back and knocked over a kayak that had been propped against the wall. But the director didn't say anything, as if she hadn't noticed the kiss. Becky helped Seth frantically right the kayak, and then the two of them raced back to the main camp.

Over the next two weeks, any time they could steal away—which had never been very often or very long at the heavily supervised church camp—he'd kissed her again. And each kiss had bound his heart closer to hers.

So now, even though it was years later, how could he listen to the logical part of his brain? He climbed out of his SUV, carried the flowers to her porch, and rang the bell.

She opened the door.

His breath caught. This was no waterlogged girl of sixteen. Snug black pants hugged her legs and a deep-blue sweater skimmed her curves. Her hair teased her shoulders in a cloud of loose, dark curls, and her eyes confidently met his.

When she looked down at the flowers, though, her cheeks turned the same soft pink that they had all those years ago. "Daisies?"

Heat rose into Seth's neck and face. "Yeah." He was thirty-one years old. He shouldn't be bringing her the same type of flowers he had when he was fifteen. But when he'd seen the bouquet at the grocery store, the white daisies had seemed as if they were made for her.

"They're beautiful. Just like...at camp." She moved back and waved him inside, her whole face radiant with a smile that proved he'd chosen exactly the right flowers.

And proved logic was overrated.

# Chapter Six

Later that night, Becky sat with Seth at a table by the fireplace at The Blue Caboose, her favorite restaurant in Columbia. Logs shifted and settled in the fire, and a jazz trio played softly in the corner of the room.

She scraped the last bite of mango vanilla cheesecake from her plate, slid it into her mouth, and made the tropical flavor last as long as possible. If she could, she'd draw out every second of this evening.

"It's weird," Seth said. "It's been years, but it feels like just yesterday we were sitting across from each other at one of those big metal tables in the camp dining hall. It's kind of surreal seeing you again."

"Yeah. I know." It was surreal. And incredibly romantic.

Seth reached across the table and took her hand, his warm fingers encircling hers.

A zing of excitement ran through her veins, just as it had when he came to pick her up and she saw the daisies. Only more so.

He stared into the fire, then looked back at her. "That summer was one of the best times of my life, and being here with you brings so many memories back. Some especially big moments..." His gaze drifted to her lips.

Her cheeks grew warm, and she glanced down. She had a pretty good idea which moments he meant.

"And other things," he said. "Like when you sang that song in the talent show."

"You remember that?"

"Every note."

"That show was so fun. Talk about best times." She'd loved being up on that stage, hearing the whole camp applaud.

Right now, though, was a pretty good time as well. She and Seth seemed to fit, almost like when she'd been a little girl and she'd formed an ideal of a fairytale prince— a man meant just for her, a man who would understand her better than anyone else, a man who would make her heart nearly burst with joy.

Then she'd met him and lost him.

And now he was sitting across the table from her.

Seth rubbed his thumb lightly over the back of her hand.

Her heart quickened, and she tried to focus on his words. Camp...he'd been talking about church camp.

She ought to ask him about this morning. Because it seemed odd that he'd chosen brunch instead of worship.

"Look at you now," he said. "A choir director. This concert you're planning... Does every performance matter this much to you?"

She slid her hand away from his and picked up her glass. "Uh, no." She didn't want to tell him why the concert mattered so much. What if he thought she was negligent, thought less of her?

But even if she didn't tell him, he'd hear. Abundance was a small town.

She took a sip of water and met his eyes. "This concert is special. I'm...hoping to overcome some problems from last summer."

"Did your choir have a bad performance?"

Her throat grew tight. "No, nothing like that." She took another drink. "Did you ever date someone who wasn't what you thought?"

Seth gave a wry laugh. "Did I ever. I was seeing this woman when I became Tony's guardian. I thought she was so special, so nice, the real deal. I was almost ready to propose."

Becky tried to look understanding. She should not feel jealous of someone from his past, but she edged forward, eager to hear the woman's flaws.

"After my brother came to live with me, I realized she was only nice if she was the center of everything. When Tony had to be a priority, things got ugly." Seth leaned back in his chair and gave Becky a look of sympathy. "So, you dated someone who was a fake, too?"

She pressed her tongue against the roof of her mouth, trying to make it less dry. "Not just a fake. A criminal."

Seth's lips pressed into a line, and an odd expression passed through his eyes.

She swallowed. Oh, she was an idiot. She should have remembered what Tony said about their dad being in prison, but she'd gotten too flustered talking about last summer. She couldn't take back what she'd said, not without explaining that she already knew Seth's secret. That would be even more awkward. The sooner this conversation was over, the better. She talked faster. "Last summer, the church spearheaded this special fund-raiser around town for the food pantry. My boyfriend took me out to dinner and said he'd wait while I led adult choir practice, then take me home afterward. While I was with the choir, he broke into the church office and stole the money from the fund-raiser."

"What a creep!"

"Yeah. He wasn't at all what I'd thought. Anyway, that's why I'm so excited about taking up a collection of canned goods for the food pantry at the concert." She wanted to make amends, and a really big food drive should be more help than the tiny financial donations she'd been giving anonymously every month.

"What happened to your boyfriend?"

"He acted like nothing had happened, drove me home, and kissed me goodnight. Then apparently went to Hershel's Grocery Store, where he was the manager, and stole a lot of money. No one figured any of it out until the next day, and by that time he'd disappeared." As if she'd meant nothing to him. As if she *was* nothing. Which was pretty much how she'd felt. "People—even people in my church—thought I knew where he was, thought I was covering for him. Susie Hershel, who owns the grocery store with her husband, didn't talk to me for two months. People even said that his theft gave the former high school principal the idea to steal from the school."

"That's not possible," Seth said. "I mean—I shouldn't tell you this—but the thefts at the high school started long before last summer."

"I'm not sure facts like that matter to certain people." Even Becky could hear the bitterness in her voice. She tried to tone it down. "The whole experience was awful. The children's choir shrank, and I even had two kids drop out of my youth choir. For a while, every time I talked to someone, I felt like they thought I was lying." Even now, that feeling hadn't completely gone away. Look how nervous she was about applying for the teaching job in Abundance. She certainly didn't want to bring that up. She was already sharing her most embarrassing moment. No need to tell him about what might be another failure.

"Why didn't insurance cover it?"

"The money hadn't been counted." She rubbed at a spot of condensation that had dripped off her glass and onto the tablecloth. "The church made a donation of $500 to the food pantry to try to make up for what was stolen, but people in town thought a lot more money had been taken."

Seth's jaw tightened. "It sounds to me like the person in charge of the money was to blame."

"Nobody saw it that way. Except my family, of course."

Seth bent toward her, his eyes serious. "It wasn't your fault."

"It feels like it was." She looked down.

"Becky, you know you'd never have let that creep inside the church if you'd had a clue what he was going to do."

"I wouldn't have." Her words echoed in her ears, defensive and a little unsteady.

"Did people even think about how he hurt you? How you'd cared about him, and he lied to you?"

"Not so much." She rubbed again at the wet spot on the tablecloth. Were her family members the only people who would really love her no matter what?

"I bet he's conned all kinds of people, maybe even folks in law enforcement. And you've got such a sweet spirit, you'd never suspect someone of doing such an awful thing. That doesn't make you guilty." He laid his hand over hers. "That makes you nice."

"Nice?" she whispered. She looked up at him.

His blue eyes filled with tenderness that seemed to flow around her.

Tension she hadn't even noticed eased in her stomach. Warmth filled her chest. Seth never would have doubted her last summer. Because he really knew her, really cared.

He squeezed her hand. "Nice," he said with conviction. "The real deal."

ᘒ

"Look at the sky," Becky said as she climbed out of Seth's car in her driveway.

He gazed up into the cold, still night. Almost all the clouds had rolled away, and the sky seemed magnified, so that each star was doubly bright, and millions more lights twinkled down than normal. The moon hung low and huge, almost bright enough to read by. And a few stray snowflakes wafted down, shimmering in the silent moonlight as if in some movie where each one ferried a tiny piece of magic to the earth.

He glanced back at Becky, bundled in a bright-red coat and candy-cane-striped scarf. Her brown eyes sparkled as she stared up at the stars.

Maybe the magic wasn't in the snowflakes. Maybe it was in those eyes.

"It's a beautiful night." He shut her car door behind her. "And I've had a great time."

"Me too." She angled her head toward the porch swing. "Would you like to sit on the porch for a few minutes and look at the moon?"

A chance for more time with her? "Sure." Though he'd rather look at her than at the moon. He took her hand and walked beside her to the porch.

"Let me get a blanket." She went inside.

He brushed snow off the swing and sat down. It had been the best date he'd had in…well, probably the best date ever. They agreed on things, even before they discussed them. And even though the woman was gorgeous, she had the same tender heart she'd had at camp.

But he didn't want to take a chance of hurting that heart. Which meant he needed to use this time together to tell her the truth. The last thing he wanted to do.

A moment later, snuggled beside her with their legs covered in a thick wool blanket, he took her hand, his big black glove nearly covering her smaller one. He gazed at the moon, searched for some cosmic sign to give him an out, to tell him to keep his mouth shut, but didn't find it. So he drew in a huge breath and turned to her. "There's some things I want to tell you. About my family. And about me."

She tilted her head to one side.

"When my dad left me and my mom, he moved to Las Vegas. He'd been gambling for years, only we didn't know it. While he was in Vegas, he married Tony's mom and his gambling got worse." Seth brushed away a snowflake that had landed on the blanket, then looked back at Becky. "He started selling drugs to pay his debts."

Her eyes grew wide, but she didn't say anything, didn't scoot away with the revulsion he'd feared.

"Four years ago, after Tony's mom died, Dad got caught. That's why Tony came to live with me." He glanced away. "And a year ago, Dad got killed in a fight in prison."

"I'm so sorry." Becky tightened her fingers around his. "For your loss. And everything. But what your dad did doesn't change who you are."

"That's only part of the story. After my parents split up, my life changed a lot. We had to move out of our house, into an apartment. I had to switch schools. People learned about Dad's gambling and…I was embarrassed. That's why—in spite of all you meant to me at camp—I never answered your email, even though I did get it."

Becky nodded, as if she understood how hard that time had been.

"After Dad left, Mom and I stopped going to church. He was the reason our family went in the first place. I mean, sometimes I think he only attended for business connections, but he was the 'Christian' that I saw every day. So, it was nice of you to invite me to your church, but…"

"You still believe in God, don't you?"

"Yeah, but God, church…it just isn't part of my life anymore. I don't really want it to be. I mean, look at how people in your congregation turned on you, and didn't believe you about the stolen money."

"People who attend church aren't all perfect, you know," Becky said. "But back to your dad, what exactly happened when he left?"

"One Friday he told me that he'd take me to a ball game the next day in St. Louis, and in the morning I couldn't find him. I thought he'd gone into work and he'd show up in time to drive to St. Louis. I kept believing that, listening to the pregame on the radio, all the way up until the first inning started. He'd gotten sick of us. He drove out to Vegas and never came back." Seth gave an awkward shrug. "If that's what Christians are like, I don't want to be one."

"Oh, Seth." Her words were tender, barely above a whisper. "Just because some believers make mistakes— even horrible mistakes that hurt their kids—it doesn't mean that's what God wants."

Was she right? No. Church, religion, Christians…too many hypocrites. He shoved his hands in his pockets. "I've been doing just fine without God."

She flinched. "Don't you feel…empty?"

How did she know? "Not if I'm busy."

"You can't fill that hole inside yourself by keeping busy. It's made for God. Deep down, you know that."

He dug his hands deeper in his pockets. He had tried to fill that emptiness with work, with women he'd dated, and—when he was in the Navy—with alcohol. It always came back.

"Maybe. Anyway"—he rocked his foot back, shifting the swing—"I wanted you to know. I really like you, but to be honest, I'm probably not a person you should date. I'm not some super Christian, and I've made some pretty bad choices."

"So have I, but God forgives us. I'm going to pray that you're able to let go of this pain and let God back in your life."

He looked at her, not sure how to respond.

She slid closer to him and laid her head against his shoulder.

Unable to stop himself, he took one hand out of his pocket and wrapped his arm around her. Sweet, trusting Becky. So naïve, believing God would make a difference in his life. Seth knew better.

And yet, in a way he envied her. In spite of all that had happened to her the past year, she still believed, and obviously still found comfort in her faith.

And she wanted him to feel that same comfort. Simply because she cared about him, because she was nice, because she was...

Becky.

They sat, side by side on the swing, gazing at the moon. Her soft hair brushed his jaw.

Without thinking, he took his other hand out of his pocket and laid it over hers, on her thigh.

She looked at him. Emotions flickered through her eyes, one after another. Sadness and sympathy and something that made him think once again of those kisses they'd shared long ago.

He pulled off his gloves and ran the fingers of one hand down her cheek, and she turned so that her body, only inches away, aligned with his.

Her dark hair gleamed. Her perfume surrounded him, sweet and citrusy, the way orange blossoms might smell. And her lips looked so soft, so inviting.

Gently, he eased his fingers into the hair at the nape of her neck.

Her eyes grew wider, and her lips opened slightly, then tipped into a smile.

His heart hammered, as fast and frantic as it had when he'd given her that first kiss so long ago. He should leave. Go home. He'd just told her they shouldn't even date. But…

He leaned forward, closed his eyes, and brushed her lips with his.

She moved closer, until their coats crushed together.

Warmth flooded his chest, and he buried both hands deeper in her hair. His past and his present and a crazy longing for the future melted together in his heart, and he kissed her again.

And again.

And again.

# Chapter Seven

Seth stretched back in his new desk chair and clicked the mouse, opening his first email. The school was still silent, with only a few teachers entering the building. Time to get his Monday morning started.

Even if he would rather think about last night, about kissing Becky.

He forced his attention to the screen, to a message about Tony from Bill Tesson. The more Seth read, the lower his shoulders sank. Spanish was not going well. Seth sent his brother a text and asked him to stop by before his first class.

Half an hour later, Tony stood outside Seth's office.

Seth gestured him in and motioned for him to shut the door. "Coach Tesson tells me you got an eight out of twenty on your last Spanish quiz."

Tony leaned back against the door with his chin jutted out. "It's not my fault. That quiz had all kinds of vocabulary I'd never seen, and he doesn't speak any English in class. At all."

"He mentioned moving you back to Spanish 1, but he thinks if you do some extra work, you can pull your grade up to a C."

Tony's chin moved forward another millimeter.

"He also thinks we should get you a tutor. Just for a month or two."

Tony raised one eyebrow.

Seth leaned forward, sales pitch ready. If Tony would work with a tutor, he probably could figure out Spanish. He was a smart kid. "The coach suggests a guy named Wayne, says he'd be great."

Tony hitched his backpack higher on his shoulder. "No way. I am not working with Wayne. Everyone will think I'm stupid."

Tony's logic seemed to be failing as well. "What are they going to think if you flunk the class?"

Tony yanked open the door and left.

Seth jerked up, about to call him back, but the bell rang.

Another parenting situation with no answer. Sure, he could force Tony to work with Wayne, but Seth couldn't make his brother learn. This was one of those problems that—if he believed in prayer—he'd turn over to God.

Where had that idea come from?

Oh. Becky.

But prayer was not how he handled things.

He glanced back at his computer and opened the email again.

Eight out of twenty.

Becky would take the problem to God. And what she'd said yesterday did make sense. Why exactly had he blamed God when Dad abandoned him and Mom?

His chest ached, even thinking about that time in his life. He had good memories of his dad from early childhood—sitting on his lap, listening to bedtime stories, practicing layups together in the driveway. But when Dad left, it had been awful. It didn't make a lot of sense, but maybe...maybe putting part of the blame on the church had made the rejection a little less Dad's fault, a little less personal.

Seth crossed his arms over his chest and studied the tile floor. Had that been what he'd done? Blamed the church to make it hurt less?

If he had, no one had ever noticed. After he and Mom moved, it had been easy to avoid people who might ask about his faith. Mom stopped going to church, and he found friends who never gave God a thought.

In high school, in college, in the Navy.

Until he ran into Becky.

Had he made a mistake in blaming God when he was fifteen?

Maybe.

And maybe he actually needed God for problems like getting Tony through high school.

He glanced out the window at the white steeple on top of the church.

Prayer couldn't hurt.

He sat for a moment, then bowed his head.

Talk about awkward. He'd turned his back on religion for half his life. How did he start this conversation?

*God? I'm kind of floundering at taking care of my brother. So if you could spare a little help, I'd, um… Please just get him through high school.*

Seth looked up, then closed his eyes quickly. He'd forgotten something.

*Amen.*

He opened his eyes. He didn't feel any different. He looked back at the steeple. Nothing. No parting of the clouds with light streaming down from above. No special glow. Just the same old church.

Maybe he needed to be patient. Things weren't always instantaneous in the Bible. He remembered that much. Those Israelites wandered for forty years. He'd wait and, sooner or later—hopefully before things got bad with Tony again—maybe Seth would get some sign that God had been listening, that he cared.

◌ʒ

Late that afternoon, Becky shook the snow off her soggy scarf and draped it over the radiator in her church office. What a day. At lunch, her principal had stopped in her classroom with news. Bad news.

Enrollment had dropped, and the school's parent advisory committee had found no solution except to cut staffing—starting with music. Next year, her position would be half-time. If—and the principal made no promises—*if* things worked out right, Becky could continue to work full-time, spending the other half day teaching the computer classes.

Talk about a terrible solution.

She sat down at her desk and stifled a moan. Now, more than ever, she needed to get the position teaching in the Abundance schools, which meant she needed a successful concert and needed to call the Catholic church.

She used the search engine on her phone to find the number but didn't dial. She didn't really want the concert to be at St. Paul's. She wanted to find a way to have it at her own church. Sure, she saw Seth's point. Having the concert somewhere else this once made it more of a community choir. But at her own church, she knew where everything was, she understood the acoustics, and she knew people—like her dad or her brother Earl Ray—she could ask to run the sound system.

Mostly, though, she was nervous about calling Father Mark.

He seemed nice enough when she saw him on the street, and he was a big supporter of the food pantry. She'd even seen a picture in the newspaper of him, loading boxes with diapers and laundry detergent and peanut butter. But would he hold last summer against her?

She blew out a breath. She'd never find a place to hold the concert if she didn't ask. Before she could change her mind, she called St. Paul's. "Father Mark? This is Becky Hamlin."

"Becky, how nice to hear from you. I ran into your cousin Abby downtown, and she told me about your plan to combine a concert with a food drive. An excellent idea."

*An excellent idea!* And she'd been afraid to call. "Thank you so much." She sat up taller. No wonder people loved Father Mark.

"The food pantry is vital to this area, especially with farm families suffering after the drought," Father Mark said. "It's horrible to think that someone would swallow their pride and go there and find the shelves nearly empty. We don't want families to end the winter having to choose between heat and food."

Claws dug into the back of Becky's throat. A horrible situation and it was her fault. If the pantry had the money collected last summer...

But it didn't. And that was the reason this food drive needed to take place. "The concert is actually why I'm calling. There's been a calendar mix-up, and we can't hold it here at our church. I wondered if we could have it at St. Paul's."

"Hmm." Father Mark hesitated, and the clicks of typing filled her ear.

"I'd be super careful with your building and make sure everything was locked up when we left," she said quickly.

"Ah, I know that won't be a problem. I'm worried about scheduling it. OSHA says we have to deal with an asbestos issue before we replace our flooring. After mid-February, our parish is attending Mass over at St. Joseph's. You know, that tiny stone church in Prattsville? We have to be out of this building the morning of February seventeenth."

"That's all right," Becky said. "The concert is scheduled for February fifteenth." This could work. Seth was right. An ecumenical approach would be a good thing. And she didn't really have any other options.

Father Mark typed again, then the phone line was silent. "I'm sorry, Becky. That weekend's out because of weddings. You know, close to Valentine's."

Her heart sank. "Oh." Her voice sounded hollow.

"Let me check earlier."

She held her breath. Earlier wouldn't be great, but with extra practices, the choir could do it. She wanted to make a difference, wanted to help. And now people were expecting the food drive. If she let Abundance down again…

"I think the church secretary's added some stuff I didn't know about," Father Mark said. "I can't really offer anything until we move back in mid-March."

Becky's heart plummeted even deeper. Her hand holding the phone shook. The volunteers at the food pantry were worried about February. The food drive needed to happen now. Mid-March was too late. And by March, the music position in Abundance would be filled.

"I'm sorry, Becky."

"Thanks anyway, Father Mark." Her voice came out high, sounding like someone else.

"I'll try to come up with another location for you. And I'll pray."

"Thank you again." She hung up and let out a deep sigh. St. Paul's was out. What was she going to do? There wasn't any other place in Abundance that was big enough to hold a concert. She might be able to find a location in Prattsville or Miller's Junction, but how many people would come? And if she couldn't find a location—

Footsteps came down the hall, and soon Abby stood at the door, coat unbuttoned, hair pulled back in her typical ponytail. Beside her, Emma licked snowflakes off her pale green mittens.

Becky dredged up a cheery expression and waved at the little girl.

"I popped in to drop off some baked beans for the community meal tonight and thought I'd say hi." Abby stopped, leaned in closer, and then walked into Becky's office. "You okay?"

"Not really. Father Mark just said our patriotic concert can't be held at St. Paul's. They're all booked up because of Valentine's Day weddings, and then they have to be out of the building—"

"For the asbestos thing. I heard about that." Abby sat down and put Emma on her lap. "But why hold the concert there? My Sunday School class already has a plan for decorating our sanctuary."

"We can't hold it here because of the parking lot. There's some dumb basketball game at the high school."

"But you told me you talked with Yvonne, got it on the high school calendar."

"I know. But somehow it wasn't there. And I got more bad news." Becky picked up a pen and twisted it in her hands.

"What?" Abby leaned forward.

"My principal told me that my position is being cut next year. Music will only be half-time. If she can work it right, the other half-day I'll teach computer classes."

"You?" Abby sounded as shocked as if Becky had said she planned to teach tax law.

"I know." Becky bit the clicker of her pen. "But I can't go part-time. Even if I found another part-time job, I wouldn't have benefits. I might have to move. And I don't want to leave Abundance. I'd have to give up everything." Her cozy little house with a mortgage that she'd have to keep paying, even if her income dropped. Her friends. Her family. And her renewed dream of a future with Seth. Tears welled in her eyes, and she tossed the pen on the desk and smeared them away. How could her life have gotten so messed up?

"You need to have that concert, so you can get the job in Abundance." Abby sounded worried. "What are you going to do?"

Emma squirmed on her lap.

"I don't know," Becky said. "Seth—you know that new principal, the one I knew from camp—he says the game can't be changed."

"He's only been here a couple of weeks." Abby laid Emma's head against her chest and rubbed the little girl's back. "Maybe there's a loophole he doesn't know about."

A flicker of hope ran through Becky. "I could talk to Roscoe."

Abby's eyes lit up. "Nobody knows the schools better."

"You're right." Becky ran a search on her phone for the number for the school administration. "I'll make an appointment. And once Roscoe finds a solution, I can help the food bank, wow Abundance with the concert, and get that job."

# Chapter Eight

Seth sat at his desk Wednesday and picked at the food on his lunch tray. The meat—and he used the term loosely—was almost the color of ham. But it didn't smell like ham. In fact, the odor gave him a whole new appreciation for the moldy stink of those old upholstered chairs. And the meat sure didn't taste like ham. It tasted like what he imagined the cafeteria workers would get if they made summer sausage. Out of road-kill possum.

The rest of the lunch on the yellow plastic tray—overcooked green beans and a roll—didn't look much better. He took a bite of the roll. Once, as a little kid, he'd eaten one of those dissolving packing peanuts made out of corn. Far tastier. Obviously, training for the cafeteria staff had to move higher on his list of priorities. Yesterday he'd called the principals at Abundance Middle School and the two elementary schools. The problem was not the quality of the food. The district had received some big grant. The problem—and one of the other principals hinted that it might be insurmountable—was the head cook, Hilda.

Seth washed down another bite of roll with the last of his chocolate milk. Somewhere, the district had to have some money to send Hilda for training. He'd talk to Roscoe. He must have heard complaints about the high school food from his grandson.

Luckily, while Seth had been in the lunchroom, Roscoe had left a message saying he'd stop by this afternoon. The perfect time to discuss Hilda.

The phone rang again. Which was about the forty-third time today.

Seth let it go to voice mail. That was another thing to mention to Roscoe—he needed a secretary tomorrow, not three weeks from now. He understood that the school board was wary, wanting an extensive background check after the last secretary had been involved in the financial mismanagement. But he needed help. Even if it was only a temp to answer the phone. Or a parent volunteer.

"Seth." Roscoe stepped into his office, pulled off his gloves, and shoved them in the pockets of his parka. "We need to talk." His tone did not sound like that of a man ready to turn over money for a temporary secretary or for Hilda's training.

"Sir? Come in." Seth rose and gestured to a chair.

Roscoe eased himself down gradually, as if he might have recently pulled something in his back. "You're not starting off on a very good foot here in Abundance."

Seth's shoulders tensed. He'd thought Roscoe supported him when he disciplined the boys for fighting. "If this is about J.W.'s detention—"

"No," Roscoe cut him off. "It's about half the town thinking you hate the food pantry." The superintendent's cheeks reddened, and the creases deepened on each side of his mouth. "Becky Hamlin came to see me yesterday. Remember, you and I talked about how community is key here in Abundance."

Seth's queasy stomach lurched. Becky had gone to Roscoe behind his back. "Sir, I don't hate the food pantry." His words nearly tripped over each other, and he gripped the side of the desktop with one hand. "I've been trying to help Becky find a solution to the problem."

"All I hear is that you're standing in the way." Roscoe's shoulders rose and lowered as he heaved out a breath. "Folks on the school board are not going to like that. You do know they can fire an interim employee with no warning, right?"

Seth's stomach drew up into a lead ball. He squeezed the edge of the desktop tighter. He couldn't lose this job, couldn't end up back in Tennessee, where Tony would fall in with the same bad crowd. "Becky had talked to Yvonne and thought the use of the parking lot would be theirs, but the concert wasn't on the school calendar." He gestured toward his computer. "When Prattsville couldn't host the basketball game February fifteenth because their gym is unsafe, I said it could be played here."

"February fifteenth?" Roscoe angled his head.

"Once we figured out the conflict, it seemed easier to find another venue for a concert than to reschedule the game. Since the concert's a town event, I encouraged Becky to call the Catholic church to see if it could be held there."

Roscoe rubbed his chin. "She didn't mention St. Paul's. And that's the night Bill Tesson told me a scout is coming to see J.W. and another boy play."

"Your grandson's got talent, has he?" Surely Seth could salvage this situation.

"Scored twenty-six points in the last game." Pride replaced the anger in Roscoe's voice. "He averages eighty-three percent from the free-throw line."

Seth's stomach eased. He released his death grip on the desk. "Those are great stats, sir. I'm sure the scout will be impressed. And I'm sure things will work out fine at the Catholic church."

"I don't see how we can change the game at this point," Roscoe said. "But you need to make sure people know you support the food pantry. You've got to impress the community and the board."

Seth glanced down at his plate. Should he wait to bring up the issue with Hilda? No, he'd never impress the school board if he didn't take some positive action. "Sir, about the food…" He gestured to his lunch tray.

"Yes, yes." Roscoe got up. "I'll let you get back to lunch. I bet it's delicious." There wasn't a drop of sarcasm in the older man's words.

Perhaps he had no sense of smell.

"You probably didn't know this, but Hilda's my wife's sister." Roscoe chuckled. "She got that recipe from Midge. Ham-and-potato casserole. One of my favorites.

It's got secret ingredients to give it that special flavor." He walked out.

Seth looked at the lunch tray and shuddered, then he glared out the window at the church, picturing Becky's face. What kind of woman a kisses a guy, tells him she'll pray for him, and then tries to get him fired?

Not a woman he wanted to be involved with. And the more he thought about what she'd done, the madder he got.

ᘓ

Becky nudged Twizzler until he leapt off the top of her piano.

He landed on the couch without a sound.

She sat on the floor, braced her feet against the piano, and pushed with her legs, rolling it a few inches closer to the wall. She stretched out her ankles, then went to the other end and evened the piano up. About four more tries and she'd have it.

All the paint in the living room was dry and looked wonderful. There was no reason not to get the room back in order.

Besides, she was too nervous to sit still.

She'd talked to Roscoe yesterday, and he'd said he'd get back to her, but he hadn't called. Last night, she'd been patient. Today, after another depressing conversation with her principal, she was even more desperate for the concert to happen.

But she didn't want to call Roscoe at home. If the game had been moved, though, Seth would know. Maybe after dinner she'd call him.

But first, the piano. She braced her feet and shoved it another few inches.

A car door slammed outside.

She stood and peeked out her muslin curtains.

Seth.

She hurried to the door and opened it before he knocked. "Oh, good! Come in. I was going to call you after dinner. What have you heard about the concert?"

"Way too much." His tone was bitter, and he came inside and shut the door. Hard.

Becky took a step back. "What do you mean, 'way too much'?"

"I mean"—he yanked off his gloves—"that I don't appreciate you going to the superintendent and trying to get me fired."

"Fired?" What was he talking about? "I would never try to get you fired."

"Oh?" His voice oozed sarcasm. "Exactly what were you trying to do when you talked to Roscoe?" He loomed over her.

She took another step back. "I thought he might have a solution for rescheduling the basketball game, some answer you might not know since you've only been here a couple of weeks."

"I thought you were going to have the concert at the Catholic church."

"We can't. They have to close for some asbestos thing and use this little church over in Prattsville for a month."

"So"—his eyes grew hard—"you decided to make me look incompetent, give people the impression I don't care about Abundance, and jeopardize my job?"

"I wasn't trying to jeopardize your job." She stood up straighter. "Which, by the way, isn't the only job that matters."

"Huh?" His eyes narrowed.

She shoved her hands on her hips. "I need that concert to show that I'm a good music teacher. And show that I care about Abundance. My position at the private school is being cut to half-time. I need to get the job here."

"What job here?"

"The music teacher for the two elementary schools is retiring."

He stared at her with his face scrunched up. Then his eyes widened and his cheeks grew red. "In order to help your career, you threaten mine?"

She glared at him. "I—"

"You never even mentioned your position being reduced when you talked about the concert."

"I only learned about the restructuring on Monday," she said. "Long after I planned the concert. And I didn't tell you I applied for the job in Abundance because I was afraid I wouldn't get it."

"Why wouldn't you get it? You're local, you've got experience, and you *obviously* know the superintendent."

"Of course I know Roscoe. And I knew he'd want to help the food pantry, but I'm not so sure he'll help me get the job. The office manager who had the money stolen from her desk last summer is his wife. She's still mad at me."

"What you're saying is that all along this concert was designed to help you get the job here in town because you're afraid people don't like you."

"No." He was twisting everything. "That was like a...fringe benefit after I had the idea to help the food pantry."

"Right." Seth sounded disgusted. "Every single thing you've done has been done out of fear. And the story you told me—where you're so altruistic and concerned about people in need—was a lie."

"It was not a lie. I do care about the food pantry." She thrust her hands out in front of her, imploring him to understand. "I've been volunteering there since last summer, making small anonymous donations, and—"

Seth's lips disappeared into a thin, tight line. "I'm not buying it. You don't really care about people in need, and you don't care about me. Be honest. Did you go to Roscoe right after you *prayed* for me?"

Becky's cheeks burned. Her hands shook and dropped to her sides. She hadn't talked to Roscoe immediately after she prayed for Seth yesterday, but pretty close. "I didn't mean to get you in trouble," she said in a small voice. "I didn't think about the fact that I was going over your head. I just thought Roscoe could help."

"Well, you're out of luck all around." Seth took a sideways step toward the door and pulled his gloves out of his pockets. "The way Roscoe talked, Tony and I are lucky we're not headed back to Tennessee. And he says that basketball game has to stay here on the fifteenth."

"Why? The—"

"There's a college scout coming in to see a couple of the boys play, including his grandson. Which means your concert is history. Like us. Stupid me, I thought we might have a future." He pulled on his gloves. "But I certainly don't need another 'Christian' in my life. Another person I can't trust." He stomped out of her house and slammed the door.

Her throat ached, and her legs grew wobbly. She edged back, until she ran into the wall, then sank to the floor. How could he think she'd lied? Think he couldn't trust her? Think everything she'd done was selfish? He didn't understand her at all.

Sure, the benefit concert might help her have an even shot at the teaching job, but she would have wanted to help the food pantry no matter what.

And she'd thought Roscoe would understand that Seth was new. But now…

Now all hope for the concert to help the food pantry was gone.

All hope for the job in Abundance was gone.

And all hope that Seth might find his way back to God, that she and Seth might have a future together was gone.

Gone. Gone. Gone.

She drew her legs up in front of her, wrapped her arms around her knees, and wiped at the tears running down her cheeks.

# Chapter Nine

Early the next morning, before the students had arrived at school, Seth spotted Bill Tesson in the hall and hurried to catch up with him. It was an ideal time to see how things were going for Tony.

"Hey, Bill, I wanted to thank you for letting Tony on the team." Seth walked alongside the coach.

"Not a problem." Bill shifted a stack of papers to his other arm.

"How's he doing?"

"I think he'll be an asset. And you know, he seems a little more interested in Spanish lately."

"Excellent." Seth's steps felt lighter. He'd bring up working with Wayne as a tutor again tonight. Maybe this time Tony would agree.

"I heard there were issues with the Prattsville game. Some concert?"

"Yeah." A concert that was a real pain. Seth kept his mouth shut on that point, but he was pretty sure it showed on his face. "It's taken care of. Becky Hamlin thought she'd arranged to use the parking lot that night, but there was nothing on the calendar. By the time she talked to me, you and I had already agreed to move the game here. It wouldn't have been right to cancel it. She was upset and went to Roscoe, but it got worked out."

"Everything's fine for the game?"

"Yes. All set."

"I really appreciate it. I've got a scout coming that night, interested in two kids."

"Roscoe mentioned that and said one of them is his grandson."

"Yeah. It could work out well for J.W. And it's even more important for the other boy. The only way he can afford college is a basketball scholarship." Bill stopped outside his classroom. "His folks have worked toward that goal for years, really sacrificed to help him succeed in sports. And I can't see them wanting him to take out a bunch of student loans."

"Well, I hope the scout is impressed with both boys."

"I think he will be." Bill stepped into the doorway of his classroom.

Seth continued down the hall. He'd done the right thing, sticking with what was actually on the calendar. Yes, the food pantry was important, but so was that game.

☙

The next day, after a Friday-night basketball game against a team from the far edge of the district, Seth walked down a dark hallway in the high school. Before he went home, he wanted to get the lunchbox he'd forgotten earlier in his office.

If only all his mistakes could be as easily rectified as forgetting his lunchbox. He'd made the right decision about the concert, but now that he'd cooled off, he could see that he hadn't handled things with Becky very well. Granted, she was in the wrong too, and she was the one who should apologize, but he wasn't proud of how he'd acted.

He let himself into his office, flipped on the lights, and picked up the lunchbox, inadvertently bumping the cup of water he'd left on his desk.

A small wave sloshed over the rim.

He grabbed his laptop and shoved it out of the way. Then he rescued a stack of papers, ran to the outer office, pulled a handful of tissues from the box the former secretary had left, and mopped up the water until the tissues were a soggy mess.

"Way to go, Williams," he muttered to himself. "You're on a real winning streak."

Once things were dry, he moved the stack of papers back in place.

A sticky note fell off the bottom of the pile. Seth picked it up and deciphered the scribble of the former principal.

*Very important. Feb. 15 saved for concert at church. Yvonne and I kept forgetting to put it in the computer, and now they've taken away our access to the system.*

Seth sank into his chair and bit back an expletive. How had he missed this? The note must have gotten stuck to the bottom of something, and he'd never seen it.

Talk about a mess. The spill on his desk and the soggy tissues were nothing compared to his life. If he'd found the note—if he'd gotten more on top of things before he made any decisions—everything would be different. The concert would have stayed as scheduled. The college scout would have planned to visit another night. Everyone would have been happy.

But what could he do now? If he left things the way they were, Becky might not get the teaching job in Abundance, the food pantry might run out of food, and she would have every right to hate him. But if he canceled the game, some Abundance kids—including his boss's grandson—might lose the chance at a college scholarship.

Shaking his head, he grabbed his lunchbox, stepped out of his office, and relocked the door.

Then—although the hallway was gated off to students during the game—a locker clanked and something rustled.

There it was again. A rustle. And this time, a giggle.

Quietly, so he could catch the culprits unaware, he set his lunchbox on the floor outside his office, turned, and inched down the hall. He stopped and listened intently. He heard nothing.

"So, I just got a text. The boys finished showering and left to get the stuff," someone whispered. "They're going out to that choir director's place—the one who hates jocks and tried to cause all that trouble for the Prattsville game."

That whisper had come from a girl. Seth could tell that much, especially after she let out another giggle.

"They're going to TP her house and block her doors."

"Really?" another girl said a little louder. "With what?"

Seth didn't wait to hear. He rounded the corner.

But before he could switch on the lights, footsteps thundered down the hall, and the girls were gone.

Great. Now he had a bigger issue to deal with than kids slipping past the gate. After his conversation with Bill Tesson about Becky...What if the coach had mentioned it to the boys? What if Seth was indirectly responsible for their plan? He'd better call and warn her, tell her to turn on all her outside lights. He reached for his phone.

Wait a minute. If the basketball team was planning to cause trouble, Tony would be in the middle of it. He was an old pro at minor vandalism. Seth let the phone slide back in his pocket. If Becky called the sheriff, it would be the last thing Tony needed. His problems in Tennessee had started out minor, but every warning from the cops seemed to provoke him and his friends to do something worse. Seth needed to make sure Tony wasn't involved before he called Becky.

He strode back toward his office, retrieved his lunchbox from where he'd left it, and headed to the parking lot. As he walked, he dialed his brother.

No answer. Had Tony ever actually picked up a call? No, that would be too convenient for Seth. "Call me," he said to voice mail. He gritted his teeth and sent a text.

Five minutes later, Seth scraped the snow off his SUV. He climbed in, waited for the engine to warm up, and checked for a text from Tony. Nothing.

Was he over-reacting? Should he go home and see if Tony was there? Or drive by Cassidy's Diner to see if his truck was parked out front? If Seth were sixteen again, that's where he'd go after a game.

No, if there was trouble, Tony was in the middle of it. One way or another, Seth needed to stop what was going to happen at Becky's.

Ten minutes later, he rounded the last bend before Becky's house and peered through the falling snow. He hit the windshield wipers to get an extra swipe and finally recognized the odd shape in the back of the pickup that blocked her driveway. A porta potty.

He parked on the road, three cars behind the pickup, zipped his coat as far as it would go, and stepped out. Snow slid into his shoe.

The snow changed to sleet. He made his way closer, using his phone as a flashlight. He didn't see Tony's truck, but he could have ridden with someone else.

Becky's house was dark, as if she'd gone to bed early. And it was after eleven.

Seth walked closer down the long driveway and saw the basketball team working together as smoothly as if executing a pick and roll. Silently, lit only by four flashlights carefully trained on the ground, one group tossed toilet paper high into her trees.

A second group had a harder job. Four boys maneuvered a porta potty onto Becky's front porch and—with only the occasional muffled thump—positioned it squarely in front of her door. A third group carried another porta potty around to the back of the house. If Seth had to guess, he'd say the one in the truck would go in front of her one-car garage.

"Not a bad plan," he said under his breath. If Becky woke up and called the sheriff, by the time the deputies arrived, the team would be long gone. And if she tried to come out to stop the boys herself, both doors were blocked, again giving them time to escape.

At least he didn't see Tony. Probably his brother had gone straight home, eaten the rest of the lasagna, and was fast asleep.

As for the boys who were here, he could handle the situation alone. There was no need to wake up Becky. Technically he was supposed to call law enforcement. But good sense said he needed to send the boys straight home just as soon as they removed the porta potties and promised to clean things up tomorrow. He could let the sheriff know what had happened later. Keeping the boys around until a deputy could arrive would only allow time for the roads to get worse.

Seth strode closer to Becky's house, and snow worked its way into his other shoe.

A figure ran around the house from the back yard, carrying a roll of toilet paper.

Heat poured through Seth. Just by the way the boy ran, Seth knew exactly who it was. His brother, knee-deep in trouble again.

With the wind whipping past him, Seth raced up behind Tony and grabbed his shoulder.

Tony spun to face him. He recoiled, and the whites of his eyes doubled in size.

Seth snatched the toilet paper out of his hand. "I can't believe you're mixed up in this, especially since it's Becky's house. Didn't you learn anything in Tennessee?"

Tony opened his mouth, and for a split second no words came out, as if his brain couldn't quite process that he'd been caught. "But I—"

"Talk about stupid."

Tony's whole face grew rigid. He wrenched his shoulder free and stomped away.

Seth squeezed the roll of toilet paper until it crumpled, and he glowered at his brother's back. No question about it, Tony wouldn't be driving any time soon. He was grounded.

Indefinitely.

03

Blood pounded in Becky's temples. She lowered the edge of the curtain on her bedroom window. She'd spotted the letterman jackets and knew all too well that her late-night visitors were members of the basketball team.

Why were they doing this? They'd gotten the use of the parking lot, not her.

She patted Twizzler's soft, fuzzy head and told him to go back to sleep. Then she spoke quietly into her phone, slid it in her pocket, and crept into the hall. Those boys weren't getting away with this. But her plan to catch them

104

would only work if she kept the lights off and if she could move into position without being seen.

Step by step, she inched down the hall toward the smaller living room window. As quietly as possible, she unlocked the window and slid it open.

Frigid air poured in.

"Hey, what's that noise?" one kid said.

Before he could raise the alarm, she reached for the nearby switch, flipped on the floodlight, and began taking photos with her phone—the perfect way to collect evidence so she could make sure each boy would learn his lesson.

But after one photo she stopped. She peered at the image on her phone, then into the yard at the person she'd just photographed.

An odd thickness formed in her brain, like a barrier that her thoughts couldn't quite break through.

Seth was TPing her house? Seth, who knew what the concert meant to her, who she'd bared her soul to about last summer?

Heat rushed into her chest. She knew he was mad about Roscoe, but this was unbelievable. Good thing her plan to collect evidence could work just as well with a stupid school principal as it would with a teenager. She clicked one more photo and shouted at the top of her lungs. "Aha!"

Seth blinked, as if still partly blinded by the floodlight.

She peered down at the photo again. Perfect proof. In the background, toilet paper draped the trees. In the foreground, Seth held a roll of TP, his eyes wide, mouth open in an *O*.

"Some responsible leader you are!" she cried out. "I've got half a mind to put this photo on social media." Talk about a post that would go viral.

Seth's face turned murderous. "I came here to stop them, not help them," he shouted. "If you post that photo, you'll get me fired for sure."

Seriously? He expected her to worry about *his* job? "You don't look like you're stopping them." Her words shot out, full of spite, but as they left her mouth, she felt a little hollow inside.

He walked closer, just a couple of feet away from the house, and gestured with the roll of toilet paper. "I took this away from Tony."

Oh. Something about his tone. Or the fact that he was wearing dress shoes. Maybe he *had* been trying to stop the boys. A lump lodged in Becky's throat. "If you're here, I guess I didn't need to call—"

"The sheriff?"

She nodded and a siren wailed, far in the distance.

His jaw went rigid and the tendons in his neck grew taut.

଍

Seth's stomach clenched. He couldn't believe Tony's problems were starting all over again here in Missouri. He glared at Becky through the window screen. It wasn't her fault, though. She lived out here alone, and she'd heard strange noises. But...

He looked back at her.

She tugged at the collar of her dark green bathrobe and closed it tighter over what looked like flannel pajamas.

Some of the boys sprinted away, but some stood frozen, watching Seth. And from near the mailbox, one boy ran closer. Johnny Driscoll.

Off in the distance, a car approached, probably the sheriff.

Seth turned toward the road.

No, not the sheriff. That was *his* SUV, driving past the end of Becky's driveway. And the only other person with keys was—"Tony!" Oh, the kid was going to pay for this. Taking his car, leaving him stranded.

Johnny came to a stop in front of Seth. "I told him not to leave in your car. He'd been trying to get us to quit, but when you thought he was involved, he got really mad."

Seth's stomach contracted. "He was telling you to quit?"

"Yeah. He said Miss Hamlin was nice."

Another boy stepped closer. "He'd checked the weather on his phone, too, and said we needed to go home because it was going to get worse."

Seth glanced at the ground, then at the branches of a nearby tree. His stomach grew so tight that he thought he might throw up. The sleet had changed to freezing rain.

Tony was driving away mad.

On ice.

The siren grew louder, coming from the east.

And then, from off to the west, the air echoed with a deafening crash.

# Chapter Ten

Becky looked west, toward the sound of the crash, but saw nothing except the dark row of cedars near her property line. The boy had said that car had been Tony, driving away.

The siren grew fainter, as if it had turned, as if it had been going to some other emergency all along. Something more serious than kids TPing a house. Where someone might actually be hurt.

Or worse. Like Tony might be.

Tears welled in her eyes, and she looked back at Seth.

His face was pale, and he stood, frozen in place.

"I'll drive you," she said. "Give me two minutes to get dressed."

But she didn't have only Tony and Seth to worry about. She yelled to the boys huddled in her yard. "Kids, move that truck out of my driveway, then come inside and call your parents. You shouldn't be on the roads when it's like this. Tell them I said it's fine if you need to sleep in my living room."

☙

Seth gripped the edge of the passenger seat with both hands and squinted ahead, searching for any sign of Tony, as Becky drove down the snow-covered road, praying under her breath. The freezing rain shifted back to sleet that bounced on the windshield and glued itself to the wiper blades.

His stomach churned as image after image of his brother flashed through his mind. Tony, grinning ear to ear when Seth bought him new tennis shoes on their first day together. Tony, laughing until tears came to his eyes the time Seth tried to cut a cherry tomato in half and sent it soaring across the kitchen. Tony, beaming as he showed Seth his new driver's license.

What if—because Seth was such a horrible guardian, even worse than his dad—what if Tony was—?

Suddenly, the car slid.

Seth braced one hand on the dash and threw the other across Becky's chest.

She steered into the skid, and the car slowed.

Seth swallowed back nausea. Tony wouldn't know to do that. Wouldn't have a clue. Seth had never taught him. Like he'd never given him a chance to say he was doing the right thing at Becky's house.

She turned at an intersection and headed toward town. Fifty feet ahead, illuminated by her headlights, tire tracks veered to the right, went off the plowed path, then reappeared across the road, as if the driver had over-corrected.

A few feet farther on, Seth's SUV sat halfway off the road, its front end smashed into a tree.

His chest constricted. "Stop," he shouted. "Let me out." He jabbed at the seatbelt release.

"Oh, Seth." Emotion choked Becky's voice, and she pulled onto the shoulder of the road.

He flung open the car door and climbed out, then stuck his head back in. "Call 911 again. Tell them where we are."

"I will."

His heart pounding, he scrambled out into the snow, skated his way across the road to the other shoulder, and ran toward the car. His gait was awkward. Sometimes one of his feet went six inches into the snow before he reached solid ground, sometimes ten. But he ran.

Then he saw his brother in the driver's seat, the airbag deployed in front of him. "Tony!"

Tony remained silent, and blood ran down his temple from a scrape on his forehead.

With a shaking hand, Seth pulled the door open. "Tony! Can you hear me?"

No response.

A cold sweat covered Seth, and he reached out to see if his brother was breathing.

Tony opened his eyes. "Hey, Seth," he said, his words drowsy and gravelly.

Seth sagged against the door frame.

Tony moaned, and his eyes shut again.

Red lights reflected in the side mirror of the SUV, and Seth raced back through the snow toward the ambulance. "Help!" he shouted. "Hurry!" He waved his arms, beckoning them closer, until the ambulance parked and two paramedics got out.

He answered their quick questions, then stood back, Becky at his side, watching them.

What was taking them so long to get Tony out?

What were they doing?

Seth couldn't help at all.

At last, the paramedics eased Tony's body out of the wreckage and onto a bright-orange backboard, then carried him to the ambulance.

A second later, just as a sheriff's car drove up, the older paramedic leaned out of the ambulance and waved Seth and Becky over. "We're ready to roll." He looked at Seth. "You're supposed to ride with us. Becky, the deputies will get your car home and take you to the hospital if you want. The sheriff doesn't want anybody on the roads."

Becky gave a small nod, and Seth climbed in the back of the ambulance.

Tony lay on the gurney, his eyes open.

Seth leaned closer. "Tony, I'm here."

His brother looked up at him with a gaze full of fear.

Seth turned to the paramedic. "Will he be okay?"

"We need to get him to the hospital to let the doctors check him out," the younger paramedic said.

A chill ran down Seth's spine. The man's tone was calm and reassuring, but he didn't answer the question.

"I was trying"—Tony's words came out thin and shaky, with pauses between each, as if he had to push each one past the pain—"to stop them."

Seth's heart wrenched. "I know. The guys told me," he said gently. "I'm sorry I assumed the worst of you."

He looked again at Tony's arm, at his leg, at his face. Sorry didn't begin to cover it.

He swallowed hard and gave Tony his bravest smile.

☙

Seth walked out of the emergency room and into the waiting room, where Becky sat twisting her hands together in her lap.

She stood. "How is he?"

He moved toward her and motioned for her to sit back down. "They're taking him to X-ray. They're doing more tests, but it sounds like he broke his left arm and right ankle and has a mild concussion. From what the doctor said, I think they're going to have to operate." He sat beside her.

"Oh, Seth. I'm so sorry." She wrapped one arm around him, halfway hugging him.

He shrank from her touch, looked down, and bunched his ski jacket against his stomach. "I can't believe…this whole mess is my fault."

She pulled her arm back and faced him. "It is not." She sounded indignant.

"I'm the one who made Tony drive away mad because I assumed he was causing trouble again."

"Didn't you say he got in trouble a lot in Tennessee?"

Seth shrugged.

"You thought what anyone would have."

"But Tony asked me to give him the benefit of the doubt. I gave him my word that I would. I failed him. I've made such a mess of things." Seth squeezed the ball of his jacket tighter.

"Don't say that." Becky's tone was so defensive, so protective of him. That was only because she didn't know the whole story.

"Becky…" He released the jacket and turned to her. "I told Bill Tesson you went to Roscoe. That's probably why the team TPed your house."

She stared at him a moment. Then she took a deep breath and blew it out. "You can't know what the boys were thinking. Besides, Tony is almost grown. He's responsible for his own decisions."

"That seems weird," Seth said. "Coming from you."

"Why?"

His mind was so overloaded that he had to think for a moment before he could explain. "I'm Tony's guardian and he's a minor, so of course I'm responsible. You can't see that, and yet you feel responsible for your *boyfriend*— an adult—stealing money. Don't you ever think that it was completely his fault, or that maybe the office manager who left the money in her desk was to blame?"

Becky's forehead tensed and she edged back. "That's different."

Yeah, it was different. He was to blame. She wasn't. But he wasn't going to argue with her. There were things he needed to say, though, starting with an apology. "Becky, I'm sorry I acted like such a jerk at your house. I said horrible things. Inexcusable things. And even worse, even if I wasn't responsible for what the team did at your house, I'm responsible for the mess with the concert." His chest tightened, but he kept going. "Tonight when I spilled water in my office, I found a sticky note from the former principal, telling me about the concert on the fifteenth. If I'd seen it earlier, none of this would have happened."

"Oh." Her voice sank.

There, he'd said it. She'd been so supportive. That was over.

She looked at the floor, then closed her eyes and clasped her hands together. After a few seconds, she raised her head. "You know," she said calmly, "I don't think we should worry about blame. We both made mistakes. Like I shouldn't have gone to Roscoe. But none of that matters now. What matters is Tony." She settled back in her chair.

"You're not leaving?"

"Because of a sticky note? No way." She put her hand on his arm, and the reassuring warmth soaked through the fabric of his shirt.

Relief flooded his chest. "Thank you."

"We need to pray." She pulled out her phone.

"You reach God on your smart phone?"

"I'm putting your brother's name on the prayer chain. More than fifty people, and most set up to receive texts. A lot of them won't see it until morning, but some want to know immediately, so they can start praying as soon as there's a need."

His prayer before hadn't seemed to do any good. But he didn't stop her. Tony needed all the help he could get.

A minute later, she held out both her hands. "Will you pray with me?"

A memory of praying with others at camp, a memory of comfort, welled up inside him. And maybe Becky was better at praying than he was. He hesitated, then took her hands, and bowed his head.

She prayed aloud, asking God to be with Tony, to be with the doctors and nurses, and to let him recover fully. She even prayed for Seth, that he could find strength in God.

Her words washed over him, and more of the tension eased from his chest. He hadn't been able to do anything at the wreck, and he couldn't do anything now. But the doctors and nurses were helping Tony. And maybe, if God was listening to Becky, he was helping too.

Seth let out a ragged breath. Maybe it was time to admit that he needed God's help, not just when things seemed impossible but all the time.

As Becky neared the end of her prayer, he interrupted her.

*"Please, God, help Tony."* His tongue seemed thick, the right words gone. *"And help me. Forgive me."*

Like a gentle wave, stretching inch by inch up a sandy beach, a feeling of peace washed though him. His shoulders sank and his eyes felt hot.

"Amen." Becky pulled Seth into her arms and pressed her soft cheek against his.

After a minute, her phone beeped.

She sat back in her chair.

It beeped again. And again. Text after text after text arrived. She shut off the sound, and they leaned together and watched the messages light up the screen. Even though it was after midnight, more than a dozen people responded to say they were praying, people who didn't even know Tony.

And Becky, who hadn't said one word about the sticky note or about her concert being canceled because of his mistake, sat by him, telling him not to give up.

He wasn't going to.

# Chapter Eleven

Seth sat beside Becky in the waiting area outside the operating room early the next morning, ripping pieces from the top of his empty Styrofoam coffee cup and dropping them inside it.

Before Tony had gone into the operating room, a nurse had told them that his surgeon was very highly regarded. Becky had stayed at the hospital all night, sleeping only briefly in a chair. And she'd prayed with Seth, again and again. He shouldn't be this scared, shouldn't have this knot in his stomach.

But the surgery seemed to be taking forever. Something might have gone wrong. Something that—

The double doors opened and a slender black man in scrubs walked into the waiting room. The surgeon.

Seth leapt to his feet.

"Tony came through the operation just fine."

Seth's breath rushed out with a shudder, leaving him limp. He reached out to shake the doctor's hand. "Thank you," he said in an unsteady voice. Then he listened as the man explained more.

"Someone will be out for you after a while," the doctor finally said. "To take you to see him." He turned and went back through the double doors.

Seth grabbed Becky's arm. "He's going to be okay."

Her eyes shone and she pulled him into a hug. "I'm so glad. Our prayers were answered."

He held her tight and silently breathed his own prayer, one of thanksgiving.

ଔ

The next morning, Becky sat in her kitchen, sipping coffee and listening to Twizzler gobble down a can of fish-and-shrimp cat food. As the caffeine hit her system, she thought back to what Seth had said at the hospital, about how she'd taken the blame for something that wasn't her fault.

He was right. She didn't steal the money last summer, didn't even know it had happened until the next day, yet she had looked at how people treated her—like it was her fault—and believed them. Maybe they hadn't even all thought that. Maybe she'd been a bit paranoid.

Because she'd been so ashamed, so hurt.

Father Mark had been fine with her using his church.

But what about Corey never letting her lock up? Was that because he got an earful from Midge?

Midge was only one person.

Becky used her phone to search the Internet for Scripture references about personal responsibility. She needed to find her answer in the Bible, not in one person's opinion. Twizzler rubbed her leg, and she put him on her lap, petting him as she read.

Again and again in the Old Testament and also in Galatians, the Bible made it clear. Each person was responsible for themselves. It had seemed so obvious when she talked to Seth about Tony. How had she not been able to see it in her own life? Talk about ignoring the log in her own eye. She really had been looking at things wrong. And that had—

Wait. She reread a line in a translation of Galatians 6.

*Each of you must take responsibility for doing the creative best you can with your own life.* (The Message)

A heaviness spread through her chest. Had she really been doing her best? When she'd ignored Abby's suggestion that she collect money as well as canned goods at the concert?

No. She'd been acting in fear. Fear of asking people for cash donations because they might say no because they didn't trust her. And acting in fear when she didn't ask Corey why he wouldn't let her lock up the church offices, when she wouldn't even tell Seth she'd applied for the job teaching in Abundance. Even during their fight, when she'd thought Seth didn't understand her, he knew her better than she knew herself. What had he said?

*Every single thing you've done has been done out of fear.*

She winced. He'd been way too close to the truth.

She didn't even need to look up what the Bible said about fear and trust. She'd memorized a bunch of those verses long ago, could recite them without thinking.

Proverbs 29:25—*Fear of man will prove to be a snare, but whoever trusts in the Lord is kept safe.*

Proverbs 3:5—*Trust in the Lord with all your heart and lean not on your own understanding.*

Psalm 37:3—*Trust in the Lord and do good.*

Trust, trust, trust. She knew so many verses about trust. A lot of good those verses did if she wasn't living them. If only she'd listened to God instead of other people's opinions and her own emotions.

She hung her head and, after a moment, prayed.

Minutes later, her chest grew lighter and she raised her head. Psalm 37:3 pretty much summed it up. *Trust in the Lord and do good.* She needed to trust that God would work things out with her job, one way or another. And she needed to find a way to help the food bank. Not partly to impress people, not because it might help her get the job she wanted, but because there were people who were truly in need.

She gave Twizzler a gentle scratch between the ears, put him on the floor, and stood up. "Time for me to get to Sunday school. And this afternoon I'll cook something for Tony and Seth and figure out what to do next."

છ

Monday at work, Becky got a text from Seth that Tony had been discharged. The minute she got home, she packed up the food she'd made the day before and drove to their apartment complex. She found the right unit and rapped softly on the door.

Seth opened it, and his face lit up. "Hi," he whispered. He held a finger to his lips and gestured to Tony, who lay asleep on a dark-brown couch, his broken leg elevated on pillows, a cup of water and his phone on the floor beside him.

"Hi, I brought you some food." She walked in and glanced around the room. It was dark, masculine, and, uh…functional. Apparently neither Seth nor Tony had figured out which channel aired HGTV.

Seth helped her take off her coat, laid it aside, and quietly said, "Becky, I don't know what I would have done at the hospital without you. You were incredible."

She put her bag on the floor. "I just sat with you. I didn't do anything special."

Seth took her cold hands in his, surrounding them with warmth. "It *was* special. You were a real friend, in spite of our problems over the concert and the ball game. I can't tell you how much that means to me." He pulled her closer and leaned in as if he was about to kiss her.

"Whoa," Tony said in a woozy voice. "I thought you two would get together. I was right."

"Tony." Seth grabbed the remote and turned on a sports channel. "Watch TV." He returned to Becky and slid his hands around her waist.

Tony ignored the TV and looked at Becky. "What sort of food did you bring?"

Seth dropped his hands to his sides and blew out a long breath.

Becky chuckled. "Lemon-blueberry breakfast bread." She pulled the bread and a plastic container from her bag and handed them to Seth. "And homemade chicken-and-rice soup."

"Lemon-blueberry bread," Tony said. "I could have some as an afternoon snack."

"You already had a snack," Seth said in an exasperated tone.

"I could have another."

"I better go put some of the bread on a plate," Seth said. "If I give him the loaf, he'll eat the whole thing in one sitting. Luckily my mom's coming later today to help. I am not cut out for nursing. It's exhausting."

Becky followed him to the kitchen. "Hey. I need to talk to you. I was thinking about what you said at the hospital, and you were right. What happened last summer wasn't my fault."

"Good." Seth pulled a plate from the cabinet. "I'm glad you see that."

"I do. I also figured out that I need to focus on my own actions and on making a difference. So I've been thinking. If you ask people to bring canned goods to the ball game, people will know you care about the community, and the food pantry will get restocked."

"No, we should cancel the game." Seth lopped off a quarter of the loaf of lemon-blueberry bread and put it on the plate. "The concert really was scheduled first. Maybe the college scout can be convinced to come to another game." He went back into the living room, Becky at his heels.

"What if he won't reschedule?" she said. "What if Roscoe gets you fired?"

"If I get fired, I'll get a job somewhere else." He handed the plate to Tony and shot him a look. "Not Tennessee," he added, with a note of warning.

"Seth, no." Becky needed to make things right, not have him give up his future in Abundance. "And what about those boys, what if they don't get a chance to go to college?"

"I don't know." Seth shook his head. "There's no good answer."

Then a commercial came on the TV, far louder than the program had been.

An odd expression came over his face. "That's it," he said in an awed voice. "That's the solution. The food bank serves Prattsville and Abundance, right?"

"Yes."

"How long is the concert?"

"Forty-five minutes."

"Excellent. We hold the JV game an hour earlier. Have that game, then the concert, then the varsity game. We can collect a mountain of canned goods."

Becky took a half-step back. He wasn't making sense. "There's no way all the people who want to see the choir and all the basketball fans from here and Prattsville can park in the lot at the same time."

"They don't need to. Like that ad"—he gestured toward the TV—"for the hotel that shuttles people to the Mizzou game. We can run school buses back and forth to an off-site parking lot."

"There's room in the gym for everyone?"

"It holds 600. All we need is an off-site location for more parking."

She inhaled sharply and stood, not breathing, as the idea sunk in. Then she let out her breath with a whoosh. "Wow, it could work."

"Let me call Roscoe to make sure there's no rule against it." Seconds later, Seth paced back and forth across the living room, the phone pressed to his ear.

Becky stood behind a recliner and leaned forward, her elbows on the headrest, watching him and trying to read his expression.

His face split into a smile, and he hung up and let out a whoop. "It *will* work!"

Electricity ran down her arms. "It's perfect!" And brilliant. A solution that had been there all along—only they hadn't seen it. As soon as she started focusing on doing good, instead of on what people thought of her, it was as if a billboard from God appeared saying "See, I've got this."

Tony shifted on the couch and closed his eyes. His breathing slowed, as if he'd fallen asleep.

Seth pulled her into his arms. He glanced at Tony and grinned. "And now, Becky Hamlin, I can kiss you without my brother interrupting."

And he did.

# Chapter Twelve

The next day Becky drove to the church lot as soon as she returned from Columbia.

Corey's and Midge's cars were in their usual spots, and the one with the Kansas license plates was gone. Perfect. The pastor had been meeting all day yesterday and today with a church consultant. But the consultant from Kansas must have left. It was time for Becky to talk to Corey. And to Midge.

Inside the church, through the window in the office door, she could see Midge's wiry gray hair. Becky knocked and stuck her head in.

The older woman looked up so fast her dangling red earrings bounced. "Becky, hi." Her tone was cool, but not as bad as on some days.

For a fraction of a second, Becky hesitated, listening to the copier in the next room wheeze as if it was running a big job, like the Sunday bulletins. Then she pulled up a chair and sat across from Midge. "Do you have a minute?"

Midge's jaw tensed, but she nodded.

Becky squeezed her hands together in her lap, chest suddenly tight. She plunged in. "That theft last summer wasn't my fault."

"Of course it wasn't," Midge said quickly.

Becky took a deep breath. She hoped she was right about this. "It wasn't yours either."

Surprise and sadness swirled in Midge's eyes, and her face crumpled. "Oh, but it was." She sounded like she might cry. "I should have put that money in the bank, but I was coming down with the stomach flu, and I just went home. I didn't even count it. But instead of blaming me, people blamed you."

The tension in Becky's chest was gone, replaced by a hollow feeling. She'd had it wrong for months. Midge hadn't been mad at all, she'd been guilt-ridden. Both of them had been miserable. Needlessly. "Oh, Midge, you can't help it that you were sick, and you locked your office." She came around the desk and hugged the older woman. "The person to blame was that creep I dated. Not either of us."

Midge sniffed and patted Becky's back. "Thank you, dear. I should have said more to defend you. But sometimes I thought people didn't want to say out loud that they blamed me, that they think I'm too old for this job, what with handling the money on the computer and everything."

Becky pulled away from Midge and stared at her. Nobody thought that, did they? She certainly didn't.

"That's nonsense. You're better on the computer than I am. Besides," she added lightly, "if you weren't here, who would tell Pastor Corey to clean up his office?"

Midge gave a small snicker. "We both know how effective that is."

Becky touched Midge's arm. "Are we okay?"

"Better than okay," Midge said, her voice warm, and she sat back in her chair.

"Good." Becky let out a happy sigh. "I need to talk to Corey too. Is he—?"

"He's in the church library. His office is..." Midge shook her head like an indulgent parent.

Becky laughed and headed toward the library.

From the doorway, she could see the library window was cracked open, letting in a chilly breeze that almost brought the temperature of the room down to normal. For some reason, the library was always too hot in the winter and too cold in the summer.

Corey sat at a table in front of the window, shirt sleeves rolled up, making notes on a printout.

Time for Round Two. Becky stood up straighter, moved closer to the table, and cleared her throat. "Corey, I need to talk to you."

He looked up. "Sure."

"How can I regain your trust so you'll let me lock up the building?"

"Huh?" He blinked and ran a hand through his dark hair.

"You always wait until I leave before you go home. Ever since last summer. I know I failed the church when my boyfriend stole the money, but can't you give me a chance? Can't you trust me again?"

Corey's jaw dropped open. "I...I do trust you." His face grew red. "Abby told me your car was unreliable, that she was afraid you might need a ride home one day, so I've been sticking around just in case."

Becky's brain went numb. She sat on the edge of the table with a thump. "Abby told you what?"

"That your car sometimes doesn't start."

"That was last summer, before Earl Ray replaced the battery."

"Really?" Corey's voice rang with disbelief and bewilderment. "Becky, believe me, I trust you. You can lock up tonight if you want. My brain can't take any more of this." He pointed to the papers and shoved them into a pile.

"Absolutely, I'll lock up. After I call Abby and ask her what she was thinking." Becky got up, spun, and headed toward her office. A minute later, she had her cousin on the phone. "Why on earth did you tell Corey he needed to worry about my car? I thought he was hanging around because he didn't trust me to lock up the church offices after last summer, and it's all you and some car thing."

"Oh." Abby's voice dropped half an octave on one word. "Well, you did have an issue with your car, and I, um, might have neglected to mention it got fixed. I thought it would help things along."

"Help what things along?"

"Help you and Corey become a couple. Remember I said he needs a wife?"

"A wife?" Becky's words came out in a squeak. "Corey's really nice, but we work together. I don't want to marry him."

"Well, no, I see that now that you're dating Seth. You two are perfect for each other. Do you think his brother will want to come to youth group?"

"Nice try at changing the subject. How would you like it if someone interfered in your love life?"

Abby gave a dismissive laugh. "I don't have a love life. My romance was years ago."

"Well, maybe it's time you had another." Abby's husband, Eric Kincaid, had been dead almost three years, and Abby definitely had romance on the brain. "I'll start working on it."

Abby sputtered.

Becky hung up.

All these months, she'd thought Corey didn't trust her. Because of Abby.

And because she'd been trapped by listening to other people's opinions and listening to her own emotions.

No more. Now she was listening to God.

☙

The following Thursday, Seth sat at his desk and loaded his messenger bag with paperwork he could handle once he drove Tony home.

Things were looking up. Becky had learned she would be one of four candidates interviewing for the teaching position in the Abundance elementaries. The basketball team had apologized to her and cleaned up her yard. A blonde girl and some of the boys on the team had stopped by several times to visit Tony in the evenings. One of the biggest drug dealers at the high school had been caught red-handed. And part of that paperwork in Seth's bag was for Hilda's retirement, effective at the end of the year. He hadn't even talked with her about training—she'd emailed him while he was at the hospital with Tony. No more casseroles with secret ingredients.

Best of all, Tony was back at school full-time and managing pretty well, his friends pushing the wheelchair that he'd need for the next several weeks. He did have a lot of makeup work, especially in Spanish, but hopefully he'd feel up to getting some of it done right away when they got home.

Seth checked the clock on his computer. Three forty. His brother should be here.

At three forty-five, Seth's phone dinged with a text from Tony.

I'm in the gym. Can I stay here for 45 minutes?

Tony was watching basketball practice? By the time his cast came off, the season would be over. He should do his homework and get to bed early. But the boys on the basketball team—though they had gone a little overboard at Becky's house—weren't headed down the wrong path like the kids Tony had known in Tennessee. Seth had heard some of those kids had been arrested for possession of LSD and ecstasy. Plus, every night Seth had been asking God to help Tony find the right path here in Abundance. Maybe God was working things out already. Seth typed a reply.

Sure. I'll pull the car around to the gym door at 4:30.

At four thirty on the dot, Seth walked in the gym, where the team was doing a shooting drill at one end of the court. Balls smacked the hardwood and swooshed through the net, one after another.

Why had he given this a second thought? Time with the team would let Tony cement friendships and would show the coach that he wanted to play next year, maybe even dress out and sit the bench or keep stats this year.

But Seth didn't see him.

Coach Tesson pointed to the other end of the court.

Becky's youth choir fidgeted on risers on the stage, and she stood on the edge of the court, wearing leggings and a long green sweater. Now that Seth saw her, he vaguely remembered putting on the school calendar that she needed the stage for something today. He gazed at her a moment. She pointed first at one choir member, then another, to move, as if she was trying to get the right arrangement on the risers.

Then he looked to the side, near the stairs to the stage.

Katiana, that blonde girl who'd come by the apartment, giggled and bent over Tony in his wheelchair, her face near his. Her honey-blonde hair brushed his shoulder.

Seth strode across the court to his brother. Tony wasn't paying a bit of attention to the basketball team. He was flirting and interrupting Becky's practice. "We need to leave," Seth said.

The girl backed away, and Tony looked up, his cheeks flushed. Embarrassment, then resentment, flashed through his eyes.

Becky walked over to Seth. "I'm so glad you're here. We're really just checking spacing, but I want you to hear the choir."

"Another time, Becky. I'm sorry if Tony has been a nuisance."

"Seth," Becky said with a note of humor. "Listen." She turned to the blonde girl. "Are you all ready, Katiana?"

The girl smiled broadly.

Seth crossed his arms, shifted his weight from one foot to the other, and glared at Tony.

Tony didn't seem to notice. He sat up taller in his wheelchair, eyes on the blonde beside him.

At a signal from Becky, the choir, including Katiana—and Tony—began to sing "America the Beautiful." Part way through, the rest of the choir fell silent and Katiana began a solo.

One by one, the basketballs stilled, and the team stopped to listen.

Then Tony joined Katiana, his strong tenor voice harmonizing with her soprano.

Chills raced up Seth's arms, and his mouth gaped open. They sounded good. Really good. Like people would pay to hear them.

A few brief lines and the duet ended in a hauntingly perfect harmony.

Tony's face lit as if he knew, like everyone else in the room, that he'd nailed it.

The choir finished the song.

One by one, basketballs began to smack the floor again.

Becky strolled over to Seth. "Now Tony can go home."

Seth walked toward his brother and tried to speak but couldn't find words.

"You should have seen your face when I started singing," Tony said.

"You were great," Seth managed to say. "I thought you were watching the basketball team."

"Nah. I won't be able to play for months. And I want to do choir."

"He's really a godsend for us," Becky said. "I only had one tenor willing to do a solo. He got that flu with the lingering cough that was going around. Tony picked the part right up."

Katiana brushed a hand across Tony's arm. "My mom and I are going to the new-member dinner at church, but she'll drop me by your apartment about seven thirty, so I can help you study for tomorrow's Spanish test. You work on those irregular verbs."

"I will," Tony said.

She said something in Spanish, her words flowing out fast and assured.

Tony mumbled something that might have been Spanish. And he gave her a look so love-struck that Seth was sure his brother would know those verbs backward and forward long before seven thirty.

Becky's words echoed in Seth's brain. She'd called Tony a godsend.

There'd been another godsend. Tony had found the right path for himself without any help at all from his older brother.

# Chapter Thirteen

Half an hour before the concert, Seth hurried into the hallway to the gym. The buttery smell of popcorn filled the air. Red, white, and blue streamers and a huge, hand-painted welcome sign hung from the ceiling.

He and Becky had publicized the concert in every way they knew how. The roads were completely clear. And, for February in Missouri, the weather was balmy.

But the number of people in the hallway before the JV game was...normal. The sound of the crowd in the gym was muted. And near the entrance, the barrel for canned-food donations looked half empty.

What could have gone wrong? If more people didn't show up, Becky would be devastated.

Becky handed the coffee can she'd been using to collect cash donations to a woman in a red sweater, the director of the food pantry. Becky hurried toward him, face tense, navy dress swirling around her knees. "My cousin Abby just texted me from the front of the school. None of the buses have arrived."

"None of them?" That explained the low turnout. Seth reached for his phone. Somehow it was on silent, and he'd missed six texts. "Wait." He scanned them. His heart beat faster. "They're on their way. There was such a crowd at the parking area that the three bus drivers had to get out to direct cars. And they say they'll have to make at least two trips each. There are about a hundred and fifty people on the buses now and probably a hundred waiting for them to return.

"The janitor told me there are two hundred people in the gym already," Becky said.

"I don't mean to eavesdrop." Roscoe walked up alongside a woman with frizzy gray hair, "but I couldn't help overhearing what you said." Pride shone in his eyes. "Outstanding job, young man, finding this solution. I was just telling my wife, Midge, here, that I expect you're going to be around for a long time as principal at Abundance High. No promises, but..."

Seth's chest swelled and adrenaline poured into his veins. "Thank you, sir." He shook Roscoe's hand with so much enthusiasm that the older man stepped back. Seth turned to Becky, but she was talking on her phone.

"Yes," she said. Her eyes grew wider. "Yes, thank you." Her face was tight with excitement, and she slid her phone in her purse.

"What's going on?" Seth said.

"That was one of the principals I interviewed with. It's not official yet, but I got the job. They wanted me to know before the concert."

"You did? That's excellent!"

"Yes!" she said, half-laughing. Then she leapt off the ground and punched the air in victory.

Roscoe and Midge beamed at her like proud parents.

"We were just saying you two are exactly the type of young people this town needs," Roscoe said. He took Midge's arm, and they strolled toward the gym.

"I can't believe it," Becky said to Seth, her voice breathless. "You're going to remain as principal, and I'm going to teach in Abundance. And if everyone brings some canned goods tonight, the food pantry should get a mountain of donations."

"Everything really is working out." And it was. Tony was singing in the choir and had gotten a B on the last Spanish test. Pastor Corey's sermons offered Seth hope and direction as he figured out his faith. And although the people at the Abundance Community Church weren't perfect, from what Seth had seen, they genuinely tried to live as Christ taught. And...

He caught Becky's hand in his. "You know who helped make it all possible?"

"God."

"Yes, God." Seth smiled. "And you."

"Oh." Her cheeks turned pink and her eyes glistened.

"Because we made tonight a success—together. Because Tony never would have found choir without you. Because I never would have gone back inside a church if you hadn't stood by me after the wreck. And because..." He ran one finger gently down her cheek. "Because I was in love with you when I was fifteen. And I'm even more in love with you now."

"Oh, Seth, I love you too," she said tenderly.

His breath grew shallow. He slid his hands around her waist and lowered his lips to hers.

She melted into his arms, into his kiss.

His heart seemed to pause—to sync with hers—then start pounding anew, even stronger.

His Becky.

His love.

The other half of his soul.

At last he edged back, his eyes fixed on her face. If he kissed her as long as he wanted, he wouldn't stop until after the concert and both ball games were over and everyone else had gone home. "I better go in and make an announcement for people to scoot closer and put their coats in their laps. I think we're going to have quite a crowd."

"I think so too."

He gazed at her beautiful face for one more second, then went into the gym.

❧

During halftime for the JV game, Becky stood at the gym door, held out the collection can to people who passed, and watched for Seth.

At last he squeezed his way out through the crowd and pointed at the food donation barrel beside her. "Wow. It's almost full."

"Check out the barrels in the back." She couldn't believe how well things were going.

Seth turned to look through a break in the crowd to where two other barrels sat, both filled to the brim. His eyes widened.

"The janitor has been bringing in a new barrel each time one gets full," she said. And she hadn't seen a fan from either team come in without adding to the pile of canned goods. Most people—as soon as they saw that she was also collecting cash—pulled out their wallets as well.

"Hey, sis," Earl Ray said as he walked up.

Emma raced toward her and wrapped her arms around one of her legs.

Becky picked her up and then was enveloped by members of her family hugging her and sliding folded bills into her donation can. She laughed and motioned Seth closer.

"You've met some of my family at church but maybe not all of them. You know my cousin Abby and her daughter, Emma." Becky angled her head toward Abby, then held Emma higher in her arms. "And this"—she pointed—"is my brother Earl Ray and his wife, Stacey, and their son, George." She gave George a special wave. "And this is my cousin Jack. His wife, Tess, is home with their new baby, Lettie, who is just the cutest thing. I never told you, but I think Tess made that mango vanilla cheesecake I had when we ate at The Blue Caboose about a month ago."

"That's her recipe," Jack said. "Probably one of the last days she worked before she started maternity leave."

Seth glanced from face to face to face, like he might not have all the names straight yet.

"Mom and Dad and Kristen and the rest of the gang are on the next bus," Earl Ray said.

"There's more of you?" Seth asked.

"You bet," Becky said. "There are a lot of Hamlins in Abundance." Her phone buzzed and she jumped. "I've got to go. It's time for the choir to warm up." She spotted the director of the food pantry coming toward her, back from taking a bag of cash to be counted. Becky handed off the coffee can and hurried into the gym.

This was it. The food drive was going great. Seth's job seemed secure. The position in the elementary schools was hers. But she wanted a beautiful concert for the town, wanted each of her choir kids to do well.

Three steps into the gym, she nearly tripped over her own feet. Hanging in front of the stage backdrop, held up by a tall, metal frame, was the biggest American flag she'd ever seen. It had to be ten feet high, and it ran across the entire back of the stage.

Coach Tesson walked over from where his JV players were warming up for the second half. "Like it?"

"I love it! Where did it come from?"

"My brother loaned it to us. He runs a flag company ever since we got back from serving in the Marines together in Desert Storm."

Becky looked from the coach to the flag and back again. "It's incredible. Thank you." Coach Tesson, the ultimate jock of all jocks, the last person in the world she would have expected to help the arts, had borrowed this beautiful flag to help her choir. Maybe people appreciated the arts more than she knew.

"Break a leg up there," the coach said.

She stretched out her arms, ready to hug him, but stopped. Coach Tesson wasn't a hugger. She could see it in his eyes. She reached for his hand and shook it. "Good luck to your boys today. Thank you for the flag. And for your service."

The coach stood a little taller and went back to his team.

Becky took one more look at the flag, then rushed to the classroom where her youth choir waited. The energy in the room was so high that it was almost a physical force. Everyone knew this would be their biggest audience ever.

Quickly, she had them warm up and run through "The Battle Hymn of the Republic," which always gave the basses trouble. Then they lined up in the hall, ready to enter the stage door. She told the kids how wonderful they looked—the boys in black pants and white shirts, the girls in black skirts, white shirts, and red and blue scarves—and assured them they would be great.

The buzzer blew, ending the JV game, and the announcer cried out, "Abundance wins, 49-38." The crowd erupted, clapping and stomping and yelling loud enough to be heard by the people who had stayed home in Prattsville.

It was time. The choir filed onto the stage, and Becky looked out into the room. Adrenaline shot into her system. The gym now held more people than she could have imagined, more people than it seemed possible to fit. To her right and her left, every seat was full in the bleachers, from edge to edge and all the way to the highest row.

"All right kids," she said. "This is it. Let's give them a show they'll never forget."

The choir did just that.

The students—even the basses on "The Battle Hymn of the Republic"—sang out strong and clear on each song. Her accompanist played like a pro. And each of the featured singers, including Katiana and Tony in their duet, did better than Becky could have dreamed.

At last she bowed on behalf of the choir and motioned to them. The ovation was thunderous.

Her heart pounded, and she gave the kids a double thumbs-up, so proud she thought she might float off the stage.

Their faces glowed and their cheeks stretched wide in smiles.

Seth climbed the stairs to the stage and motioned for the microphone. "I have numbers," he whispered.

She handed him the mic.

He quieted the crowd. "Ladies and gentlemen, because of the generosity of the people of Prattsville and the people of Abundance, the director of the food pantry that serves both our towns has been flat-out stunned." He paused, waiting until the anticipation in the room was palpable. "You brought food, diapers, and other needed supplies that filled almost four 50-gallon barrels. And you contributed more than three *thousand* dollars!"

Members of the audience drew in their breath, then applause and cheers rang out.

Becky's eyes grew hot, and the back of her throat prickled. Oh, these people, these wonderful, generous people. She reached for the mic.

Seth moved it away from her and continued speaking. "Becky Hamlin has told me that future concerts of the Abundance Youth Choir will also be benefits for the food pantry. I'd like you to join me in thanking the woman responsible for bringing us this beautiful concert and for helping the food pantry today and in the future." He gestured to Becky, handed her the mic, and gave her a huge grin. Then he walked to the side of the stage.

The applause was so loud that the very walls of the gym seemed to vibrate.

Her chest swelled, and she wiped tears from her cheeks. The people of Abundance loved her choir, and they loved her. Seth had helped her to see it, and—though his own faith had been faltering—had helped her to listen more closely to God.

"Thank you," she said, voice wobbling. "We have one more song today to celebrate our presidents, our country, and our freedom. Before we begin, I'd like to ask everyone who served in the military to stand."

One by one, men and women scattered through the bleachers rose. Near the doors, a couple of veterans who were standing stepped forward. Becky saw people stand up that she knew had served, like her Uncle Will, Coach Tesson, and Roscoe Grange, but also dozens of people she had no idea were veterans—a woman who worked at the post office and a local insurance agent. And, like the veterans in the doorways, Seth moved forward.

"This one is for you," she said. Then she gestured to the audience. "Ladies and gentlemen, please join us in singing 'God Bless America' as a thank-you to our veterans."

The piano began, and the choir members lifted their voices. Then the audience joined in, people rising to their feet without prompting and thundering out the words. The music soared, echoing into the rafters of the gym with their enthusiasm.

Becky gazed across the stage at Seth, her heart overflowing with more pride and love than she ever thought possible. Their future in Abundance looked bright indeed.

# Epilogue

*Four months later, May 30*

With every new month and every new day, came a chance to begin a new chapter in life. With the person you were meant to love all along. Or the person you had loved and lost—and found again.

At least that's what Seth hoped.

He stood at the edge of the parking lot shared by the church and the high school, and waved at a truck from a local landscape service that rumbled away into the steamy spring evening. He glanced over at his brother, breathed a prayer of thanksgiving for Tony's healing, and handed him a package of seeds. "Time for us to get to work."

CB

Becky bent down to look at the ground in front of her car. Yesterday, between the sidewalk and the edge of the parking lot shared by the church and high school, there had been a strip of grass, spotted with a few dandelions dancing in the sun. This morning there was only dirt, as if the sod had been removed and the earth plowed.

She straightened up.

A tall man in a navy shirt strode across the parking lot from the high school, a man she'd recognize anywhere. Seth.

"Do you know what's going on here?" She pointed to the ground.

"I do." His blue eyes twinkled, and he pulled something from the pocket of his tan pants. "This." He held out a small paper package.

She took it and read the label. *Shasta Daisy. Perennial.*

"Tony and I were out here planting past dark last night. We never would have gotten it done if I hadn't hired someone to remove the sod as soon as you left after choir practice, and if Katiana hadn't held a flashlight at the end."

"You mean it's all daisies?"

"I thought you might like them." He sounded amused and nervous, all at the same time. "And I hoped you might like something to mark where we met again here by the church, to remind you that you're loved by God and"—he held out a small velvet box—"by your husband."

The air seemed to catch in her lungs, and she raised a hand to her chest.

Seth looked down at her, eyes tender with love.

Her legs felt weak, her arms shaky.

He opened the box and there, surrounded by daisy petals, was a diamond solitaire. "Becky Hamlin, will you marry me?"

Her heart filled with so much joy that it felt as if it might burst. She gazed up at his face, so handsome, so dear. "Yes!"

He slid the ring on her finger and drew her close.

Warmth swirled into every corner of her heart. God had blessed her beyond belief. This man, this wonderful man, who had won her love with a bouquet of daisies from a field when she was sixteen, now held her heart completely. She raised her face to his, and kissed the man meant just for her.

And his love merged with hers in perfect harmony.

# A Note from the Author

Dear Friend,

Thank you so much for reading this novella about Becky and Seth. I hope you enjoyed it!

This story isn't modeled after real life, but one aspect of it is close to my heart—the idea of a couple with a shared past falling in love. Although my husband and I didn't date until we ran into each other in our late twenties, we'd known each other since before we started grade school. There must be a million ways to fall in love, but I know from experience that it can happen quickly when you already know someone well.

If you enjoyed this story, I would greatly appreciate it if you would take a moment to rate it and write a review on Amazon or Goodreads. Those reviews are the best advertising around, and you wouldn't believe how fun it is to get feedback!

If you'd like to receive an email when my next book is released, please sign up at www.sallybayless.com.

Two other books in this series are available on Amazon: *Love at Sunset Lake* and *Christmas in Abundance*.

If you'd like to say hello, you can email me or find me on Facebook or Pinterest through links on my website.

May God bless you,

Sally Bayless

# ACKNOWLEDGMENTS

Huge thanks to everyone who helped me write this book!

First, thank you to the people who answered my questions about basketball, medicine, music, and food pantries. Dr. Janice Huwe, former Division I basketball player (Brown University '89) and high school assistant basketball coach, was invaluable. She not only reviewed all the references to basketball, but also beta-read the entire manuscript. Her husband, Robert A. Holm, Jr., D.O. FACEP, reviewed the medical issues in this story. M.V. Freeman, a fellow author and an R.N., helped me figure out how to handle some places where my writing goals and medical facts collided. Elementary music teacher Michele Karoub-Holzschu helped me with all things related to music. Michael Bila, who serves as a church representative to the board of a rural county food pantry, answered my questions about food pantries. I can't tell you how grateful I am to these people who shared their expertise. Any mistakes that slipped in are errors on my part.

My dear critique partners, authors Susan Anne Mason and Tammy Doherty, offered excellent suggestions as always. Thank you both!

I am blessed to have a wonderful group of beta readers that made this story so much stronger. Big hugs and thanks to Michelle Blackwell, Kristina Gerig, Diann Graham, Jan LeBar, Leisa Ostermann, Carrie Saunders, Stephanie Smith, and Diana West.

Sally Bradley was my developmental editor. As with each of my previous books, she pushed me to go farther and make my story better, and I couldn't be more grateful.

Thank you to the wonderful Christina Tarabochia for copy editing this story. Her excellent suggestions and encouragement were invaluable.

Kim Killion made the beautiful cover. Thank you, Kim!

Thanks to my dear family—Dave, Michael, and Laurel—for all your support and encouragement.

And finally, thank you, Jesus, for being with me in my daily walk and on my writing path.

# ABOUT THE AUTHOR

Sally Bayless was born and raised in the Missouri Ozarks and now lives in the beautiful hills of Appalachian Ohio. She's married and has two nearly grown children. When not working on her next book, she enjoys reading, watching BBC television with her husband, doing Bible studies, swimming, and shopping for cute shoes.

Have you read the companion novella to
The Abundance Series?

If not, please turn the page to read the beginning of

## *Christmas in Abundance*

# Chapter One

The last thing Lanie Phillips needed to hear was Christmas music.

She jabbed the button of her car radio and cut off a chorus of elves singing "The Most Wonderful Time of the Year." Wonderful? Not likely, considering she'd be spending it alone.

The wail of the wind intensified, and her headlights reflected off pellets of snow that whipped across her line of sight. She pulled her wool scarf higher around her neck. Even with the car's heat on high, the cold seeped in. She squinted through the squall of white, wishing for some indication that she was nearing the Mattox place. Finding her way down the county roads outside her hometown of Abundance, Missouri, was bad enough in the dark without adding a snowstorm into the mix.

Around the next bend, a small sign barely stuck out over the snow. "You're almost to the Mattox house!" it read.

She gave a silent cheer.

Hand-painted holly leaves and candy canes curled around the red and green lettering. Maybe Kelly, her boss, had been planning a big Christmas party. Whatever the reason for the sign, Lanie would take any help she could get to find the right house.

After another half mile, she rounded a curve and found a second sign: "Please park only on this side."

Kelly Mattox must have had some party in the works. Lanie could only imagine how flustered her boss must have been, canceling a party and leaving town unexpectedly.

Up ahead a mailbox read "Mattox" in reflective, stick-on letters.

"Finally." Lanie turned into a snow-covered gravel drive. To her right a small house sat close to the county road. Her destination was farther back, the two-story farmhouse at the end of the drive.

A tall figure jogged toward her, and the skin tightened at the base of Lanie's scalp. She had no intention of making the headlines. No plans to star in "Missouri Art Teacher Murdered While Pet-Sitting for Principal." She locked her doors and kept driving.

The figure waved, and a man's face, now illuminated by a flashlight, appeared near her window. He shouted something. Did he say her name?

Lanie eased to a stop and lowered her window.

"You're Lanie, right? Uncle Rich said you were coming." He reached out a hand in a large black glove. "I'm Kyle Mattox."

Oh. Her boss's nephew. He should be safe. And he sounded friendly, with a hint of the northeast in his voice. "Lanie Phillips. Pet-sitter." She stuck out a mittened hand.

He gave it an enthusiastic shake.

Kyle was tall and thin, from what she could tell under his bulky red ski jacket, and he had wavy brown hair and a narrow face. His mouth quirked to one side like he was on the verge of a chuckle, and his eyes were the color of dark-roast coffee. Lanie could see kindness in them and a resemblance to her boss's husband.

She drew back her hand—perhaps a second later than she would have if she hadn't been staring at his knit cap. And its foot-long antlers.

This was her straight-laced principal's nephew?

"I live in the guest cottage with my daughter." He pointed to the small house at the end of the driveway. "I'm glad you're here to take care of Jellybean. My schedule won't let me be home enough."

Lanie glanced toward the cottage, then looked back at his cap and counted five jingle bells on each antler.

"Man, I bet Aunt Kelly gave you three pages of typed instructions." Kyle shook his head slightly, as if Kelly was lovable but a bit loony.

"Actually, it was four." Lanie couldn't keep the amusement out of her voice.

Kyle grinned. "She spoils that dog rotten."

Even though the chocolate lab was pregnant, Kelly had gone a little overboard. Lanie really didn't need all those instructions, as she had often helped her grandfather, a veterinarian, when she was younger.

She gave a rueful smile and moved a finger toward the power window button. The wind gusts were freezing, scattering snow over her face and the inside of her car.

"Daddy?" A young girl who looked like she was in kindergarten or first grade peeked out the back door of the cottage.

"I got it, April," he called back. Then he looked at Lanie. "I've been fixing one of the breakers. For the light show."

"Light show?" She released the control, leaving the window halfway up.

"Yeah, the Mattox Christmas Light Show. Since Uncle Rich has to be gone, I told him I could run it."

Judging from Kyle's tone, this was an honor akin to lighting the Christmas tree at Rockefeller Center.

"Didn't you notice the signs?" he asked. "People drive out to see it."

"They do?"

"Aunt Kelly didn't tell you?"

"Not a word."

If Kelly had mentioned it, Lanie would have stayed at her apartment and told her boss to find another pet-sitter. A bunch of cars going up and down the county road, honking at each other, did not sound like the perfect writing retreat Kelly had promised. But being somewhere different for the holidays, even just across town, had sounded good, like it might take her mind off things.

Because Christmas was wonderful, but…not always. Not six years ago. And not this year. Friends had invited her to spend the break with them, or just to come over for the big day, but she'd declined. She knew herself too well, knew she'd feel horribly awkward.

"April, hit that switch I showed you," Kyle called toward the girl. "We'll check the breaker."

Halfway up the drive, a trio of snowmen, each about eight feet tall and outlined in white lights, came alive and danced from side to side in rhythm to some unheard melody.

"Thought I'd fixed it." Kyle's voice held a note of pride.

"Oh, they're cute," Lanie said. Not worth driving seven miles out of town in the middle of winter to see, but festive.

"That's nothing." Kyle turned toward the cottage. "Flip the big switch, sweetheart," he yelled.

Behind him, eight reindeer began flashing, two by two. "Rudolph, the Red-Nosed Reindeer," performed by some '40s crooner, blasted from speakers in the yard.

Lanie cringed at the sound, then followed the flashing lights, glancing from the reindeer on one side of the drive to a ten-foot Santa on the other, as if watching an electronic tennis match.

"And that's just the beginning," Kyle said. "We have fourteen Christmas trees, sixty-two giant snowflakes, 'Happy Holidays' spelled out on the roof of the cottage, three more snowmen, and eight dancing gingerbread boys." He waved his arms, indicating features hidden by the darkness, listing each with emphasis, like a car salesman showing the top-of-the-line model. "Thousands of lights in the oak trees and—over by those pines— Mary, Joseph, and baby Jesus." He angled his head to point, and one of his antlers flopped over, making the bells jingle. "All lit with fifty thousand lights, activated in time to music on a fifteen-minute loop."

She stared, mouth dry, until "Rudolph" ended and Santa and the reindeer went dark. An off-key rendition of "Deck the Halls" screeched from the speakers. A circle of Christmas trees formed from lights and wire began flashing, one after another, in a pulsating, nauseating spiral, like some out-of-control carnival ride.

It was Christmas—bigger, louder, and tackier than Lanie had ever imagined. The antithesis of the holidays she was used to—tussling on the carpet with her nephews, sipping cocoa with her mom and sister, and watching her brother-in-law untangle all-white lights for a real tree.

Lanie turned back to Kyle and blinked, still seeing halos where her retinas spasmed from the lights. Even the first few notes of some holiday songs made her chest ache. And then there was the noise—the show completely short-circuited her plans for a peaceful winter break. How could she write while subjected to this?

"I did a bunch of rewiring last night to fix the sequences on those." Kyle waved toward the circle of Christmas trees. "I'll have to tell my new buddies in IT that it worked. Man, they are so jealous of this setup."

Lanie opened her mouth, then clamped it shut.

"I know, you hardly know what to say, it's so cool," Kyle said.

Lanie raised her window. The only way this would be cool was if the Mattoxes had a soundproof room in the back of the house. With blackout curtains.

Her back teeth pressed together, she gave a short wave and drove toward the farmhouse.

Kelly probably had her hands full watching her twin two-year-old grandsons while her pregnant daughter was in the hospital. Lanie didn't want to make things harder. She knew how medical issues could be overwhelming—she'd been there when Mom had gotten sick. But she had to finish her thesis before the break ended or she wouldn't be graduating.

She couldn't take the dog to her apartment.

And she couldn't work here.

First thing in the morning, she would send a text to her boss and gracefully bow out of this nightmare.

Surely Kelly could find some other dog lover who would appreciate Christmas on steroids.

**This book is available in e-book and paperback on Amazon.**